IF HOUSES, WHY NOT MOUSES?

*Why we say what we say
the way we do*

by

Damian O'Brien

 **New Generation Publishing**

About the author

Damian O'Brien is a former racing driver with a degree in Oriental Studies from Oxford University. He has lived in Siberia, Libya and Saudi Arabia and currently divides his time between Iraq and Bulgaria. He doesn't have a favourite word, but he quite likes the sentence *dō-midēdum smakkabagm glaggwuba*, which means *we judged the fig tree exactly* in Gothic.

Tristram, said he, shall be made to conjugate every word in the dictionary, backwards and forwards the same way;-every word, Yorick, by this means, you see, is converted into a thesis or an hypothesis;- every thesis and hypothesis have an offspring of propositions;-and each proposition has its own consequences and conclusions; every one of which leads the mind on again, into fresh tracks of enquiries and doubtings.- The force of this engine, added my father, is incredible in opening a child's head.- 'Tis enough, brother Shandy, cried my uncle Toby, to burst it into a thousand splinters.

The Life and Opinions of Tristram Shandy, Gentleman (Laurence Sterne)

CONTENTS

A note on scripts, translations and languages

In the main text, words from languages which do not use the Roman alphabet are given in romanised form with the form in the original script following in brackets. In quotations the order is original script first, romanised second, and English translation third. This applies to words from Arabic, Modern Persian, Urdu, Sanskrit, Russian, and Ancient Greek. (The term Greek always refers to Ancient Greek.) Gothic is presented in standard transliterated form (slightly modified Roman). Due to the difficulty in obtaining adequate fonts, Old Persian, Avestan, Old Chuch Slavonic and one word in Hittite are simply rendered in Roman script. A few additional characters are used in romanised forms for sounds specific to particular languages viz: Sanskrit *ḷ* and *ṛ* represent full vowel forms of *l* and *r*; *ḥ* is for the word-final aspiration known as *visarga*; *ṣ* and *ṭ* for retroflex sibilant and stop; and *ś* for the palatal sibilant. Old English *æ* represents the vowel sound in the word *cat*; *þ* and *ð* both represent *th* (voiced as in *then* when intervocalic, otherwise unvoiced as in *thin*). Gothic *þ* is for voiceless *th*; *d* when intervocalic or as final after a vowel is for voiced *th*; and *ƕ* is for *hw*. Vowel lengths are shown in romanised forms of all languages except, by convention, Latin (unless directly relevant to the analysis) and titles of texts (except Sanskrit ones). A reconstructed or unattested form is prefixed with an asterisk. Translations from all languages are my own and are intended to illustrate the linguistic point under discussion. They neither aim for nor achieve eloquence.

INTRODUCTION

Another book about the history of language?

The western world's interest in language and languages tends to reflect wider preoccupations. The enormous growth of psycholinguistic research since Chomsky and the popular appeal of books such as Stephen Pinker's *The Language Instinct* reflect the modern fascination with how we think and learn and communicate. Then, for more hands-on linguists these days the challenge lies in documenting obscure languages being squeezed out of existence. Extinction is always grimly gripping but perhaps we more keenly sense it now that environmental catastrophe looms over entire regions and hunter-gatherers are being chased out of the last untouched depths of the jungle.

From the mid-eighteenth to the early twentieth centuries the administrative demands and commercial and evangelical opportunities of empire shaped linguistic research by stimulating the study of African and Asian languages. The roots of linguistics as we know it are in the academic pursuits of the soldiers, civil servants and missionaries of the colonial era. As most of them had learned Latin and Ancient Greek at school, their interests naturally extended beyond the modern languages required in their professional lives to the oriental classics. It was here that the extent of the connections between Latin, Greek, and Sanskrit, the literary language of ancient India, became clear. This was the starting point of Indo-European studies, of the comparative study of languages, religions and mythology. Historical philology determined the direction of swathes of anthropological research up to the present day, but in time was overshadowed by the new branches of learning it helped create. If optimistic orientalists dared to dream that Sanskrit may one day be widely taught in British schools alongside western classics, that dream was dashed by the end of empire in the mid-twentieth century.

This golden age of philology, in which the light of Sanskrit illuminated the structural profundities of related languages, also found in the dead Germanic language of Gothic the solutions to some of the biggest problems of English phonology. One of Victorian England's most brilliant philologists wrote in 1888 that, "A knowledge of Gothic ought to be as common among Englishmen as it is now rare." It was an extraordinary hope that has never come close to fulfilment.

There is a vast literature in Sanskrit and hardly anything in Gothic. Sanskrit was the language of the gods, while Gothic was a fruity thing spoken in bits of Bulgaria by a revolting crowd normally associated with the decline of the Roman Empire. What they have in common, however, is that they are generally perceived as belonging to some great obscurity. Sanskrit grammar and Ancient Germanic philology are bywords for the arcane and esoteric. This is not without some justification. I was placed first in my year in my final exams at university. I was also placed last. I was the only student entered for a Sanskrit degree that year. My second subject was Ancient Iranian and no undergraduate had been examined in that since a member of the nobility sixteen years earlier. So scarce was up-to-date research into Ancient Iranian philology that knowledge of French and German, in which much of it is written, was a *sine qua non*, and I was once given an essay reading list recommending an article in Japanese. Later, if I mentioned to anyone that I had taken up the study of Gothic the response was usually, "I didn't know you were interested in architecture." As for writing a book about it all....

These languages, the distant zenith of their scholarship, and the seemingly high number of pathologically eccentric obsessives that they attract can all seem somehow rather remote. Actually they are but a heartbeat away from something whose widespread appeal and modern popularity are built on their firm foundations. That is etymology. Stories about the origin, meaning and development of words are rarely without some amusing detail. I remember when I was a teenager one Sunday lunch at which a Jesuit classicist visiting from the Vatican remarked that there probably wasn't a single verb of motion in Ancient Greek which couldn't also mean to have sex. Etymology is fun, but it can seem like just so much froth and it generates rather a lot of books at trivia level. These feature vignettes of word histories which tend to focus on the development of meaning. Changes of form and the reasons for them are often treated only briefly. Yet changes of form are responsible for the most obvious differences between languages, and an awareness of them is very practical be your interest casual or serious.

As a perennially popular field etymology is vulnerable to the opportunistic cash-in. Some time ago a notorious halfwit called Bill Bryson wrote a criminally ignorant book on English replete with moronic observations and hoary drivel. The sloppiest example of the latter was the notion that Eskimos have lots of words for snow. This idea is fully debunked by linguistics professor Geoffrey Pullum in his book *The Great Eskimo Vocabulary Hoax* (clue's in the title, Bill). Bryson – one of whose books a reviewer predicted would sell well chiefly because there was no shortage of idiots - was later made Chancellor of Durham University, which was a bit like asking Dan Brown to be the Pope.

The aim of this book is to bridge the gap between the arcane and the froth. On the one hand etymology is given substance when placed in its true context as one strand of the rich process of language development. On the other hand the broader, deeper discipline of comparative philology is not so arcane that its principles cannot easily be appreciated from seeing examples of language in use. This book is concerned with features of linguistic history as far as they relate to modern English – why we say what we say the way we do, and how we know.

It is divided into sections which deal with some of the more important, interesting and illuminating areas of form and meaning, with the focus on form. The first section looks at a few individual sounds and how their evolution has caused English to develop differently from other languages. The patterns involved are not complicated. They provide a basis for understanding how languages can change and hence how words in different languages are related. They help us to rule in what is important and rule out virtually everything else. The first section also looks at the phonological background to some apparent inconsistencies in modern English. It is here we see that the history of English sounds is one thing, and the history of English spelling quite another. Our focus is on sound.

The second section moves on to meaning and examines some verbal roots. These are the underlying monosyllables which have generated most of the vocabulary of modern English. Because they are often well obscured in modern English it is instructive to look not just at how they became so, but also how they developed in related languages that later exported words to English, a process which has had a hugely multiplicative effect on the size of the lexicon.

The third section combines sound and meaning to focus on the development of some nouns, and gives examples of how man's response to the natural world stimulated the growth of vocabulary. The fourth section section is a miscellany.

This is not cutting edge linguistics. It is intended to be informative without being technically dense. Simplified (non-standard) renderings of reconstructed forms are used to highlight specific sound changes and because laryngeals and the finer points of Proto-Indo-European phonology are beyond our scope here. Phonetic symbols are not used as the range of languages cited would require rather more than the average reader may be familiar with and thus obfuscate rather than illuminate. If you are a purist and find yourself offended by this approach, get əʊvə ıt. The standard alphabet is deviated from only where necessary and in

3

ways that should not send readers scurrying for additional reference materials. The reader should also be aware that when we speak of languages, from Modern English to Ancient Greek, these are or were dynamic tongues of numerous dialects spanning several centuries. People say things and spell things in different ways for many reasons. Forms cited here are those found in standard dictionaries or edited versions of literary texts.

We are primarily concerned here with streams of change that have fed Modern English. Understanding, for example, irregular verbs in Modern English is impossible without seeing how they functioned in Old English. Fully understanding the Old English system is difficult without seeing the same system better preserved in Gothic. Though the Gothic is beautifully clear, it nevertheless offers only a reduced version of an older system best understood through Sanskrit. Hence quotations from other languages are used to illustrate relationships to English. Examples are contextualised so that someone encountering one of these languages for the first time can clearly see similarities in use as well as form. I have endeavoured to stick to solid facts, and where there is not substantial agreement on something I hope that much is clear.

That should, and I hope does, make for an interesting read. For some a grasp of an old language or an understanding of word formation in English is sufficient in itself. But where else does this knowledge take us? At the time of writing in 2012 government funding for the humanities, into which category falls anything philological, is due to be withdrawn from universities in much of the UK. So, is there a broader point in studying the history of languages?

What have old languages ever done for us?

In his authoritative guide to Indian epigraphy Richard Salomon cites an estimate that around 80 per cent of our knowledge of Indian history before A.D.1000 has come from inscriptions. That's an awful lot of history that might otherwise be unknown to us had some chap in the eighteenth century not sat down one afternoon and traced out the squiggles on a rock that nobody had paid much attention to for aeons. India has vast literatures in many languages recorded after A.D.1000 and also before, reaching back through the oral tradition into the second millennium B.C. But history was not a primary Indian genre. There is philosophy, poetry, science, drama, epic, religious writing. There is all that archaeology can tell us about the age and origin of physical remains. But there is neither diarist nor chronicler, none such as Herodotus or

Tacitus in the Graeco-Roman tradition. (At least, none yet found.) Inscriptions, though, are primary sources of information about daily life. Salomon reckons that were it not for inscriptions we would know virtually nothing of the history of the Gupta dynasty, the greatest northern Indian empire of the classical period.

In the mid-eighteenth century a remarkably resourceful Frenchman called Anquetil du Perron (whose middle name was, remarkably, Hyacinthe) was the first European to attempt a translation of the sacred books of the ancient Persian Zoroastrian religion from the original Avestan. Better-trained philologists initially assumed his ropey translations to be indicative of forged texts. But closer comparison of the language with its far more extensively documented eastern neighbour Sanskrit showed that the versions available to du Perron, though themselves depleted and corrupted, were based on texts of genuine antiquity. If a figure called Zarathustra ever existed it was now possible to estimate where he was from and when he might have lived, and to clarify the form and meaning of the words attributed to him. Over two thousand years after the emergence of one of the world's pioneering monotheistic doctrines, after the religion had all but vanished from its homeland, and after the language of Persia had changed beyond recognition, philologists found themselves looking at information lost to Zoroastrian culture for centuries, providing a crucial reconnection of identity and values which could not have come from anywhere else.

Jean-François Champollion's decipherment of the hieroglyphs on the bilingual Rosetta Stone in the early nineteenth century was a momentous event. It marked the very dawn of modern Egyptology, a discipline which has established Pharaonic Egypt as arguably the most spectacular and widely known of ancient civilisations. A few years later Henry Rawlinson completed the decipherment of the Old Persian cuneiform on the great trilingual rock inscription at Behistun in western Iran, which stimulated the decipherment of the accompanying texts in Akkadian and Elamite. This crucial phase of oriental research culminated in a discovery of immense significance.

British archaeologists had begun toiling in the cradle of civilisation itself, in the place where myth and religion and history began – Babylon. The nearby city of Nineveh in what is now northern Iraq is a few hours' drive from the Mountains of Ararat in southeast Turkey, said by the Book of Genesis to be where Noah's ark came to rest when the great flood ended. In 612B.C. Nineveh was thoroughly sacked, and the enormous library of the Assyrian king Assurbanipal – a few decades earlier the most powerful man in the history of the world up to that point – torched. Two and a half thousand years later when Austen

5

Henry Layard unearthed the remains of the library, he found the fire had actually baked and helped preserve thousands of clay tablets which constitute one of the greatest surviving collections of ancient Near Eastern writing.

By far the most sensational find turned out to be a series of tablets inscribed in Akkadian telling a story now known as the *Epic of Gilgamesh*. This was translated at the British Museum in London by George Smith, a self-educated Assyriologist who had left school at fourteen. It included a more ancient version of the Old Testament flood story. The discovery of this episode in *Gilgamesh* complete with a character named Utnapishtim who was clearly the original Noah, was astonishing to a European culture which for centuries had imagined the Bible the ultimate source of these tales. It is said that when he first realised what he was reading, Smith tore off his clothes and ran around screaming. In terms of composition the Bible was shown to be just another book. It had borrowed from a jumble of sources some of which predated all Abrahamic religious culture. This only a decade or so after Charles Darwin had unveiled a theory of the origin of species which showed that *Genesis* could be no more than just another creation myth. Smith (fully clothed) presented his findings to an audience which included the Prime Minister William Gladstone.

The survival of any of these things is quite incredible. Virtually everything is lost. The library at Nineveh turning into a giant oven for clay tablets is an exceptional example of fire not being an entirely maleficent force. Nineveh had inspired the great library at Alexandria, part of which, according to Plutarch, was accidentally incinerated in 48B.C. by Julius Caesar. The single surviving copy of the epic poem *Beowulf*, one of the cornerstones of Old English literature, narrowly escaped destruction in a fire in 1731 in Westminster. It sustained considerable damage which has caused deterioration ever since.

Still the finds continue. In the early 1990s, in an episode of excruciating mystery, the British Library came into the possession of some items discovered in the Afghanistan-Pakistan border region. This area had once been part of the ancient kingdom of Gandhāra on whose western edge lay the city of Bamiyan. Bamiyan became notorious in 2001 when the Taliban dynamited two massive sixth-century Buddha statues after days of target practice with anti-aircraft guns. What the British Library had acquired was a collection of birch bark scrolls stored in clay pots and believed to be the oldest examples of Buddhist texts ever discovered. Estimated to date from the first century A.D. these are roughly contemporaneous with the Dead Sea Scrolls, which were similarly stored in jars for nearly two thousand years. Both the Buddhist

Scrolls from Gandhāra and the Dead Sea Scrolls from Palestine have illuminated our understanding of the way religious people thought during crucial periods in world history. Now we can look at words written by the hand of someone who actually belonged to the Dharmaguptaka school in the early days when it was instrumental in spreading Buddhism outside India, and of someone belonging to a messianic sect near Jerusalem at the time of Christ.

Rigorous philological analysis of ancient texts cuts through the layers of distorted interpretation accumulated over time. If you want to know what a text really means, you are certainly better off consulting a philologist than a priest, imam or brahmin. Followers of any book-based religion usually agree that their book somehow contains the unquestionable message of their god. But they often find it surprisingly difficult to agree among themselves on what that unquestionable message is. This calls to mind the words of the sixteenth century French scholar Joseph Justus Scaliger: "All religious strife arises from the ignorance of grammar." Because of philology we can actually read, understand, repeat to ourselves in their own language, and ponder what people believed before everything began to change.

The scarcity and irreplaceability of these items makes them disproportionately valuable. They have had enormous cultural implications, transforming our understanding of the origins of fundamental ideas and identities. These texts also touch us as individual readers in an age when daily more and more trivia pile up on huge digital information storage devices. After the people have died and their cultures crumbled, after the gods have been killed, and the prophets ignored, their words twisted by the appetites and circumstance of each passing generation, these fragments of consciousness remain to show us that there is no dream undreamt, no salvation unyearned for, no folly unindulged, no beauty unnoticed since the beginning of time.

These ancient texts demand our attention because they have survived when so much else has faded. That attention is amply rewarded, and the first step is to understand how the languages work. As we share cultures and ideas with ghosts of history, so we share words too. By understanding what the words meant and how they were used we can start to feel why people used them the way they did. That is as close as we can get to actually hearing their voices.

Why and how do connections exist?

There are many theories of the origins of language. We may never know where or how language first emerged but spoken communication of a form resembling our notions of language must have existed for at least tens of thousands of years   before the earliest surviving records from a handful of millennia ago. What is clear from those records is that by four thousand years ago there had developed numerous highly complex languages which were mutually unintelligible. It is therefore impossible to deduce actual features the original 'language' had, or at what point it began to change. We may suppose it had nouns, for example, but we do not know what any of them were. More and less batty attempts have been made to reconstruct an ur-language but we will never find any evidence of it.

We can, however, examine the languages we do know of and classify them in families according to their mutual resemblance or lack thereof. The family with the greatest number of languages is probably the Niger-Congo family of which Swahili and Zulu are some of the most widely spoken. Arabic and Hebrew share many features which identify them as Semitic languages. Semitic languages form a large subgroup of the Afro-Asiatic language family, which also includes such things as the Somali spoken in the Horn of Africa and the Berber found in the Libyan Sahara. English was originally a mainland European dialect spoken in coastal areas of what is now Germany, which identifies it as a Germanic language along with German, Dutch and others. Germanic languages are a large subgroup of the Indo-European language family, the family with the greatest geographic reach. If you travel west from the Chukotka region in the far northeast of Russia through northern Asia into Europe and over the Atlantic across America to Alaska, which is separated from where you started on Russia's Pacific Coast by only the few miles of the Bering Strait, you would hear Indo-European languages all the way (unless you traversed Siberia in the company of monolingual Eskimos and insisted on visiting Finland).

The furthest back we can go with hard evidence in linguistic history is to the earliest members of these families. The oldest records of Indo-European languages are Bronze Age texts in Hittite and Mycenaean Greek. Attempts to reconstruct a parent language of this particular family – rather than of all language ever - have met with some success. Proto-Indo-European is a corpus of forms likely to have been the basis of all Indo-European languages, although we shall never find any written evidence of it. The forms posited by this reconstructive work provide a theoretical norm by which it can be measured how and to what extent descendent languages have deviated from a likely original. By identifying elements which have remained constant, we can then see which elements have changed. For example, the sound *tr* is common to the way people have said the number 3 for thousands of years. In Sanskrit the word is *t-ri* and in Latin *t-res* and in French *t-rois*. But in English *th-ree* the voiceless plosive *t* has become the voiceless fricative *th*. If we then transpose this change onto other words we find it a regular phenomenon. Thus a verb meaning to become dry appears in Greek as

t-ers (τερσ) and Sanskrit as *t-r̥ṣ* (तृष्) but in English as *th-irst*. Such a pattern, even cursorily examined, should suggest that the English form is non-original. English is a West Germanic language, and if we compare the English form *three* with the East Germanic Gothic form *þ-rija* (where *þ* = *th*) it becomes clear that *th* is not simply an English modification but a pan-Germanic one. It is part of a series of sound changes known as the First Germanic Consonant Shift. (A subsequent development in German itself, the High Germanic Consonant Shift, changed the initial *th* to *d* to form *d-rei*.)

This is proof that these words in these languages are related and are subject to certain changes in certain circumstances. It is one example of the gradual changing of a sound which contributes to the divergence of one language from another, and as these changes continue over thousands of years the divergence continues too. However, sound change is not the only reason why connections between words can become obscured.

The alphabet – a good idea at the time

Language is sound. Writing is an attempt to represent this sound. English uses a writing system adapted from the alphabet used by the Romans to write Latin. The Romans had in turn adapted the alphabet used for the ancient Etruscan language of central Italy. The Etruscan alphabet derived from the Cumaean system used by Greeks in a colony north of Naples. The Cumaean alphabet was based on the Greek, which in turn derived originally from the Phoenician alphabet used in Asia Minor. The Phoenician may have its origins in the Proto-Sinaitic script that was used alongside hieroglyphs during Egypt's twelfth dynasty nearly four thousand years ago.

Three of the languages just mentioned that have used variants of this same writing system – Phoenician, Etruscan, and English – are completely unrelated to each other. Phoenician was a Northern Semitic language of the first millennium B.C. and belongs to the same family as modern Arabic, which is also written in a Phoenician-derived script. When Etruscan died out around the first century A.D. it was an isolate language completely unrelated to any of its neighbours. (But in one of those astounding episodes of linguistic history which seem about as probable as a visit by Martians reciting Shakespeare, the sole copy of the longest of the few extant texts in Etruscan – an undeciphered text known now as the *Liber Linteus Zagrabiensis* - survived only because it was written on linen later used in the mummification of the corpse of Nesihensu, wife of a Theban tailor in Ptolemaic Egypt. The mummy was bought around two thousand years later in 1848 in a market in Alexandria by a Croatian bureaucrat who kept it in his living room.) And English is a Germanic language of the Indo-European family which includes such diverse things as Icelandic in far northern Europe and Urdu in Pakistan.

So, despite the immense gaps in time and space the characters used to write this Modern English word in the anglicised form of the Roman alphabet

television

and the characters used to write the same word in Modern Arabic (borrowed from English and pronounced very similarly, *tilifizyon*)

تلفزيون

all derive from the same ancient system, which was not designed for either. The Arabic and the English have diverged to the point that none of the letters used in *television* resemble any of the letters used in تلفزيون. Further, while the written form of the English word contains five vowels, the written form of the Arabic gives no clue that between the consonants *t, l, f,* and *z* there are any vowels at all, let alone three or that they are all *i*. Perhaps most notably the English reads left to right while the Arabic reads right to left as the Phoenician did.

Despite now being, for all practical purposes, completely different, both Arabic and English letters are still listed similarly to the original Phoenician. The first two letters in the English alphabet – the Greek *alpha* and *beta* of *alpha-bet* – are also the initial *alef* and *baa* of Arabic. (Moreover the *–bet* of *alphabet* is a word of Phoenician origin. Originally the Phoenician letters were acrophonic, which is to say that the name of each letter is a word starting with that letter. So the Greek form *beta* comes from a Phoenician word meaning *house*, which survives as a common Arabic word for *house - beit* (بيت)). Common sequencing also occurs roughly halfway through modern alphabets, with *k l m n*, the Greek *kappa lambda mu nu*, which is *kaaf laam miim nuun* in Ara-

10

bic. The order of these letters seems, however, totally random. The vowels are scattered, and homogeneous pairs - *t* and *d*, *p* and *b* – are separated. Moreover the breathing represented by the letter *h* – a letter which performs several other functions in English spelling, as in *chicken* and *physical*, as well as apparently none, as in *night* and *honest* – appears in the midst of all this despite being neither vowel nor consonant. It is as though instead of the sequence 1, 2, 3, 4, 5 there were instead 1, 23, 167, 3, 10½. A logical sequence of sounds or sound symbols may not be as obviously desirable as a logical sequence of numerals, but it nevertheless doesn't have to be this way.

Much of the world adopted from Indian mathematicians a system of writing numbers now widely known slightly erroneously as Arabic numerals. The world could have looked at what Indian scribes were up to as well. Their *brāhmī* letters – which may also ultimately derive from Phoenician - developed into the *nāgarī* forms used to write languages such as Sanskrit, Hindi and Bengali. In these systems the sounds of the language are logically grouped according to their place and organs of articulation. While English-speaking children learn their *a b c*, Indian children learn their *k kh g gh* and their *p ph b bh*. For some reason the users of Phoenician-derived writing systems west of India resisted this approach, and not because it hadn't occurred to them. The eighth century Arabic philologist al-Farahidi composed a great lexicon entitled *Kitāb al-'Ayn* listing Arabic words not in the haphazard Phoenician order but starting with the sound *'ayn* produced very low in the throat, and finishing with *miim* produced at the lips i.e. from the furthest back place of articulation to the furthest forward à la *nāgarī*. Yet we, in the twenty-first century A.D., still retain and use on that most modern medium the internet chunks of alphabetic sequences which may have first been carved into rocks on the Sinai Peninsula and noticed by visiting Phoenicians in the nineteenth century B.C.

The Phoenicians must have nevertheless developed a good system. The intention seemed to be for one character to represent one sound, which made it easier to manipulate than the comparatively cumbersome hieroglyphic and cuneiform scripts that had thitherto flourished. Indeed the spread of the Phoenician system coincided with the decline of these two older forms of writing. The languages which adopted it contained different or additional sounds, and so the process of tinkering began which has brought us to today's Roman and Perso-Arabic and Cyrillic systems.

But English and every other language which uses Phoenician-derived scripts have long outgrown them. The English alphabet lists five 'vowel' letters – *a e i o u* - but there are many more vowel sounds.

One written English letter can represent several different sounds. Compare the pronunciation of the letter *o* in the words *box*, *stone* and *bullock*. Inversely, one sound can be represented by several different letters or combinations of letters e.g. the vowel sound represented by *o* in *stone* is represented by *oa* in *load*. These inconsistencies have provided the impetus for theories of spelling reform based on the actual sounds of a word. These theories are a practical response, but they fall down for various reasons. Languages are continuously changing and when the pronunciation of a word changed so too would the spelling need to. The pace of language change may have slowed a little since Johannes Gutenberg's breakthrough with printing in the fifteenth century, which has been probably the biggest factor in the standardisation of languages in all history. But printing has also had a hand in dooming further spelling reform, especially in English. The relationship between the form and pronunciation of many words is peculiarly complex compared to German or Hindi or Italian. Meaningful reform would have to not merely alter but transform the appearance of much writing. Would we have to respell all the words in every book ever printed lest they become inaccessible for future generations unfamiliar with the old system? Attempts have nevertheless been made in other languages to clarify the relationship between a word as we see it on paper and as we say it.

Russian orthography was reformed shortly after the 1917 revolution and the changes were successfully implemented by virtue of the government's control over the printing industry. In other places and times it has not been so straightforward. In 1996 the governments of Germany, Austria, Liechtenstein and Switzerland agreed to implement a commendably practical plan of spelling reform which aimed to clarify both the pronunciation and derivation of words. One outcome was that triple consonants are now a feature of compounds. Where previously *Fluß* (where *ß* = *ss*) + *Schiff* + *Fahrt* would be written *Flußschiffahrt*, it is now *Flussschifffahrt* (meaning *river navigation*). The reforms suggested that *ß* be restricted to representing *ss* after long vowels only – the vowel in *Fluß* is short – and double consonants be restored in composition so that compounded forms were written identically to uncompounded forms. However, the reforms were strongly opposed and even now have not been fully adopted. Although obligatory in education and public administration, the country's supreme constitutional court ruled that outside of these spheres people could spell however they liked.

The invention of the International Phonetic Alphabet (IPA) in the late nineteenth century responded to the need for a way of representing sounds that provided a more accurate guide to pronunciation than existing written forms. By then the Roman alphabet was dozens of centuries old and, as we have seen, originally designed for a completely unrelated language. The IPA, and similar English-specific phonemic alphabets, have made the monstrous complexity of the English spelling-pronunciation maze more accessible to those willing to learn their dozens of symbols, but there are obvious limitations. The phonology of English varies from one region to another. The English spoken in central Glasgow is substantially different to that spoken in rural Cornwall, let alone Ohio or Delhi. The phonetic transcription included in a dictionary entry does not represent Glaswegian or Cornish and is thus only a guide. It describes how a word may be pronounced by a speaker with a standard English accent, which excludes virtually all native English speakers not only in the UK but the world. The sentence, "My house is big" looks (and sounds) more similar in Italian and Spanish - *la mia casa è grande / mi casa es grande* – where you pretty much say what you see, than if we were to respell it according to how a Cockney and a Scotsman might say it - *mee yairss iz big / maa hoos uz beg*.

Because the sounds of a language are more dynamic than its writing system, any widely spoken language with a range of dialects (and without additional means of differentiation such as a pitch accent system like Chinese languages have and Indo-European languages used to have) will struggle to avoid homophonic and homographic relationships arising between unrelated words. Unless we properly understand what we are looking at and hearing, we are therefore susceptible to....

The pitfalls of etymology

The speech organs of one human function in the same way as those of the next. When I speak English I do not click like the Xhosa speakers of South Africa or roll my *t* and *d* like a Tamil speaker in India, but I could if I practised. Sounds possible for humans to produce belong to a finite range, so inevitably sounds found in one language are also found in others. As with discrete sounds so with syllables, so with pairs of syllables, and so sometimes too with longer strings of syllables. Sounding similar, or even the same, in different languages does not a meaningful connection make.

Related languages have cognate words. These share common ancestors and can be linked through established patterns of sound change which allow us to transpose correspondences onto not merely a single word but an entire lexicon. At once a great deal is illuminated and many speculative questions of associations between words that simply look similar can be eliminated as irrelevant.

Sometimes words are borrowed from unrelated languages, and these can be confused with similar-looking native words. When I acquired a Siamese kitten a few years ago I did some research on the breed and found that the first Siamese to win a UK cat show in 1898 was called *Wankee*. This name looks rather like a later English word to which it cannot possibly have any relation. There is no normal, or moderately abnormal, reason to connect the activity denoted by the English word with a Victorian cat, whatever its habits and however handsome it was. If Mrs Robinson's *Wankee* the champion cat was the source of the English word, it would have been the first – and given its subsequent connotation quite possibly the last – time the cat-fancier community had supplied a new word to the world at large. There is also the matter of the gap of about fifty years between *Wankee* the cat and the emergence of the English word. If someone wanted to coin a word for that sort of thing that would resonate in the 1950s, they surely wouldn't choose the name of a long-dead cat. They would choose the name of a well-known post-war cat or – as seems more likely - not a cat's name at all. Despite all this, despite there being nary an iota of evidence that *wank* and *Wankee* are related, and despite *Wankee* being an entirely respectable utterance in Thai, the name of that first champion cat has not been passed down by British catbreeders.

The *Wankee* example shows up some of the problems of randomly linking words across languages. There has to be a reason for a connection to exist. A word may have passed from one language to another through commercial or military or artistic interaction. It may have been appropriated and its form or use or meaning altered completely, but there will be an evolutionary trail of those changes. The forms of the words have to have more in common than similar spelling or pronunciation in their current states. If two words in unrelated languages happen to sound the same now, we must not forget that these states were arrived at after centuries in which each word passed through numerous stages at which they may have looked and sounded nothing like each other. False etymologies often completely ignore this rather obvious fact, they ignore long-established rules of historical sound change, and generate implausible theories based on fanciful associations of meaning (although *Wankee* seems to have been a leap too far for anyone). They also tend to overlook the problems that most people can't pronounce foreign words very well, are likely to spell foreign words wrongly, and compensate for a word containing a sound that does not even exist in their own language by swapping it for whatever sounds about right – all of which would likely make it completely unrecognisable to a native speaker of the word's original language.

The pitfalls of etymology are nowhere better expressed than in Yule and Burnell's *Anglo-Indian Dictionary*. Its authors documented how words from Arabic, Malay, Tamil, Mandarin, Persian, Hindi and so on had passed into English during the colonial period in whose twilight they were writing. The scope for sound mangling, spelling confusion, and rampant false etymology was great. In the entry for the word *tiffin* they deftly refute a theory that the word is of Sinitic origin, pointing out that "anything whatever may be plausibly resolved into Chinese monosyllables." In other words, it can be made to look Chinese, but it is really about as Chinese as *chopstick*.

PART ONE

Sounds

Anyone who has played the game Chinese Whispers knows that the sounds of speech are easily altered in transmission. Between a Glaswegian and a Cockney on mainland Britain there is probably as much variation in how certain individual 'sounds' are pronounced in their common language as there is between a Sudanese and a Qatari on different sides of the Arabic-speaking world. As words gain affixes and become more complex, original sounds can be affected by sounds in new neighbouring syllables. There is a tendency to harmonise adjacent sounds to make words easier to pronounce. This triggers a divergence from unaffixed forms of the same word. Or a particular adjacent sound may act as a block to changes which would otherwise occur. Indo-European languages tend to eat themselves. Elements coalesce in fast speech, sounds harmonise, and syllables collapse into each other in a constant process of elaboration and reduction. The illusion of irregularity created by these evolutionary divergences is convincing. But beneath the surface the diverse threads of sound can be rewoven despite thousands of years and thousands of miles of separation.

1.1

N

If *goose*, why *gander*?

Many forces have acted upon English as it has evolved from one thing to another. The Celt, the Roman, the Norman, and the California Valley Girl have all left their flavours on our tongue, even as its export to distant regions has generated variations such as the Spanglish of the Americas and the Hinglish of the Asian subcontinent. Then there is the distinct contribution of the Ingvaeones, a bold tribe of mud-eating coastal paddling folk tied into their winter underwear all year round, whose linguistic legacy echoes yet in every type of English on earth. But who were they?

Their name surfaces in a description by the Roman historian Tacitus of some tribes in the coastal region of the Netherlands and Lower Saxony. Reporting that their mythical progenitor was known as Mannus, he continues:

>   **manno** *tres filios assignant,*   *e quorum nominibus*
> To **Mannus** they assign three sons, from whose names

>   *proximi oceano* **ingaevones**,   *medii*
> the coast tribes are called **Ingvaeones**, those of the interior

> *hermionines, ceteri istaevones vocentur.*
> Hermionines, and the others Istvaeones.

The coastal Germanic dialects - Old Frisian, Old English and Old Saxon - are hence known as Ingvaeonic or North Sea Germanic. That few English words end in *–nth* is due to the habits of the Ingvaeones. Before we look at these habits there are some red herrings to be cast back into the North Sea.

We are looking here at words which would have ended in *-nth* in prehistoric Germanic languages. So, the ending of ordinals such as *ninth* and *seventh* do not count. This is a late development which took place only in the last thousand years or so. The Old English forms did not end in -*nth*. Old English dropped the final -*on* of numbers such as *nigon* (*nine*) and *seofon* (*seven*) and replaced it with -*oþa* to make *nigoþa* (> *ninth*) and *seofoþa* (> *seventh*). Likewise the Modern English word *month* does not count because it occurs in Old English as *mōnaþ* - very similar to the German *Monat* - and its contraction to *month* must also have therefore happened quite recently.

A similar-looking word does, however, fall into our purview. In proto-Germanic there was a word **munth* which was pronounced rather like our Modern English word *month*, but its meaning was not *a period of four weeks or so*. This **munth* became the Modern German *Mund* and Modern English *mouth*. The Ingvaeones dropped the nasal -*n*- of **munth* and lengthened the preceding vowel to create the Old English *mūþ*, pronounced with an -*oo*- in the fashion that persists in some Scottish accents. (The Great Vowel Shift, which transformed original English sounds into their more complex forms, then produced the modern English pronunciation, for more on which see 1.3.) That this treatment was peculiar to Ingvaeonic is clear when other Germanic forms are compared. Old Frisian, like English, has *mūth*, but the eastern Gothic has *munths*.

The same process turned Proto-Germanic **tanth* into Old English and Old Frisian *tōþ* > Modern English *tooth*, contrasted with the Modern German *Zahn*. The original **tanth* is related to the Sanskrit *dant-* (दन्त) and the Latin stem *dent-* which yields words such as *dent-ist* and *dent-al*. This divergence is also seen in Proto-Germanic **anth-ara* becoming German *and-er* (and is found in Sanskrit as *ant-ara* अन्तर) but Old English as *ōþ-er* (> Modern English *oth-er*).

Having established the basic process – loss of *n* and compensatory lengthening of the preceding vowel – if we cast our net a little more widely we find that this process is not confined to the combination -*nth*. At first glance, there is no reason to think the English word *goose* and the Sanskrit word *haṃsa* (हंस meaning *goose*) are related at all. In fact they have a common ancestor.

Let's delete the final -*a* of *haṃsa*, which simply indicates that the word belongs to Sanskrit's thematic noun class, and focus on *haṃs-*. Then let's be a little more precise about the spelling, which in Sanskrit dictionaries tends to be altered for orthographic convenience from its original *haṇs-*. If we then harden the *h* sound in the throat we get something like *kh*. This produces, alongside the Sanskrit *haṇs-*, a form **khan*, which is the basis for the Greek *khēn* (χήν), which means *goose*.

The Latin form *ans-er* dispenses with the initial aspirate but is otherwise identical to the Sanskrit. Old High German had the word *gans*, which is the form found in Modern German dialect. We therefore have:

Sanskrit *haṇs-*

Latin *ans-*

OHG *gans*

Just as Proto-Germanic **munth* went into German as *Mund* but into English as *mūth* with a long -*oo*- to compensate for the loss of *n*, likewise *gans* kept its *n* in German, but entered Old English without it and with a longer, rounded vowel sound, giving the form *gōs* (whose vowel would have sounded like that in "he *goes*". The vowel later changed to the -*oo*- sound of the modern word).

Similarly the English pronoun *us* (Old English *ūs* pronounced *oos*), which is identical in its Ingvaeonic brethren the Old Frisian and Old Saxon. This contrasts with the short vowel and/or retained nasal in other languages such as Gothic and German *uns*, Hittite *anz*, and Latin *n(o)s*. In addition to –*nth* and –*ns* a third combination subject to this process was -*mf*. This is seen in the contrast of Gothic *fimf* and Old English *fīf* (> Modern English *five* contrasted with German *fumf*).

This is all because the Ingvaeones found the combinations -*ns*, -*nth*, and -*mf* at the end of words not to their taste. They dropped the nasal and lengthened the preceding vowel. This is known as the Ingvaeonic nasal-spirant law, the spirants being the *s*, *th*, and *f* sounds following the nasals *n* and *m* in the above combinations. It is important to understand that it is only these combinations that were involved in appreciating why the feminine form of *goose* is *gander*, which may otherwise seem an irregular mutant. Actually *goose* is the form that has gone astray, and *gander* is more faithful to the ancient Germanic *gans*. How? The original form was *gan-dra*. (Or, more precisely **gan-ra* - English had a tendency to insert a *d* after *n* in this sort of position, which accounts for the French *gen-re* beside the English *gen-der*, and the German *Donn-er* beside the English *thun-der*.) Because the *n* in *gan-ra* was not followed by either of the spirants *s* or *th* the Ingvaeones saw it and thought it was good.

Regarding the meaning of the words in this section, we know what *us* means. *Mouth* is an etymologically quagmirical. Different theories have suggested links to the Latin verb *mandere* (to *chew*), the Sanskrit

20

verb *math* (मथ् to *eat*), the Latin noun *mentum* (*chin*) and the Sanskrit noun *mukham* (मुखम् *face / mouth*). As for geese, the Greek suggests a connection between *khēn* and the Greek root *khain-* meaning *gape*. This accords with the Old English verb *gān-ian* which yields the word *yawn*. Yawning doesn't distinguish them much from other animals, so the connection with this verb is a bit tenuous. *Other* from **an-thara* is actually the comparative form of *ān* which is the Old English number *one* (see 4.1).

We can have a decent bite at *tooth*. The Latin and Sanskrit versions *dent* and *dant* were present participles, the sort of thing that in English would end in *-ing*. (A clearer example is the word *mut-ant*, from the Latin verb *mut-are*. A *mut-ant* is something that is different, that is changing or, as we now use the term, has changed. The word *wi-nd*, the English relation of Latin *ve-nt-us*, is also originally a participle of a verb meaning *blow*.) However, *dent* and *dant* and have actually lost a crucial initial sound which would illuminate the word's origin. Because the accent of this word originally fell on the vowel of the suffix, represented in the Latin as *e* and Sanskrit as *a*, the initial unaccented vowel dropped off. It did so at a very early stage, and it is unusual to find a form of the word with the initial vowel preserved. Greek retains it in *od-ous* (ὀδούς) and its more recognisable stem *od-ont-* (ὀδόντ-), which is used in compounds such as *orth-odont-ist*. The whole thing started off as **ed-ont*, the present participle of the verbal root *ed*, which crops up in the Latin-derived word *ed-ible*, and the verb *eat*. But for that accentual accident and the Ingvaeonic nasal spirant law, we might talk not of a *dentist* looking at our *teeth*, but *edentists* looking at our *eatanths*. So the words *eat* and *tooth* both come from the same ancient utterance, but the only common remnant is a solitary *t*.

1.2

H

How *capital* and *head* come from the same word.

Just as members of the Ingvaeonic subgroup developed features distinguishing them from other Germanic languages, so the Germanic group as a whole diverged from its continental neighbours. As a consequence it is difficult now to discern how there could have ever been a relationship between the English word *head* and the Portuguese word *cabeça* - despite them both meaning *the globular thing that you peer at the world from* and both deriving from the same word.

The First Germanic Consonant Shift is the highly regular transformation in western European languages of certain Indo-European consonants. For example, the sound *k* in the parent language became a heavy breathing *h* in Germanic languages. If we apply this to the Latin stem *capit-*, meaning *head*, we get **hapit*. A little more tweaking takes us to the Gothic stem *háubid-* (compare the modern German *Haupt*) alongside the Old English *hēafod*. By the Middle English period, the medial consonant *f* was fading away to leave a word variously spelt *hede* and *heed*, which eventually came to be written *head*. Meanwhile, in Portugal, immune from Germanic consonant shifting, the Latinate form with initial *k* sound and medial consonant intact was mostly retained, hence the modern *cabeç-a*, alongside Italian *capo*.

The same shift from *k* to *h* explains the link between *heart* and *cardiac*, which comes from the Greek feminine noun *kard-ia* (καρδ-ία). A parallel neuter noun is *kēr* (κῆρ) which looks rather like the Latin *cor*, which goes into French as *coeur*. However, the rest of the Latin declension has a final *d* – for example, the ablative plural meaning *from hearts* is *cord-ibus*. The nominative singular *cor* lost its *d* due to a tendency to simplify consonant clusters at the ends of words. The *d* also occurs in Sanskrit where the initial sound is fully aspirated and the

word appears as *hṛd* (हृद्). However, the phonetic rules of Sanskrit do not permit words to end in -*d*, so the *d* only appears as the stem final when there is a case ending attached. For example, the ablative plural, again meaning *from hearts*, would be expressed by the form *hṛd-bhyas*

22

(हृदमयस्). The correspondence to Latin can be seen thus:

```
c   or  d   -i-  bus
h   ṛ   d   -    bhyas
```

Aside from our c/h shift the main difference is that Latin has added to the consonant-stem noun *cord-* the connecting vowel *i* before the inflectional ending. This was imported from the i-stem class where, as the class name suggests, it was not a connecting sound but the part of the actual stem e.g. *turri-s / turri-bus* (*tower*).

In Sanskrit's uninflected nominative singular the final *d*, rather than disappearing as it does in Latin *cor(d)* and Greek *kēr(d)*, becomes instead the unvoiced equivalent *t*, giving the form *hṛt*. This is starting to look very much like the modern English *heart*, which appears in Old English as *heort-e*. The k/h interchange of the Germanic and Romance forms *heart* and *coeur* is exploited by Shakespeare in the following lines from *Hamlet* where he juxtaposes *heart* and *core*. These have similar meanings but have not been conclusively proven to be cognate, although Shakespeare's paraphrase *heart of heart* in the same line suggests that he may have considered them so:

Give me that man
That is not passion's slave, and I will wear him
In my *heart's core*, ay, in my heart of heart...

A common Sanskrit word for *friend* is the bahuvrihi compound *su-hṛt* (सुहृद्) - *one who has a good heart* (the *su* prefix of *su-hṛt* is related to the Greek prefix *eu*, as in *eu-logy*).

The same forces are at work in obscuring the link between *hoard* and *custody*. The Latin *custos*, meaning *guardian*, is another example of a word with a simplified final consonant cluster. The full stem is *custod-*, which we see in the related English forms *custod-ian*, *custod-ial* and so forth. If we isolate the root *cust-* and set it next to the Gothic verb *huzd-jan*, we see that the k-h process has occurred here too. The Gothic verb means *store up*, and is related to the Old English *hyd-an* (Modern English *hide*) through the sequence:

huzd-jan > *hud-jan > hyd-an

where the *u* of the root becomes *y* due to a process called i-umlaut (see 1.3) caused by the *j* of the infinitival suffix *-jan*. From this derives the

23

noun *hord* and thence *hoard* - something that really needs a *custodian*. In the noun *hord* the Gothic sibilant *z* in *huzd* has been regularly changed to *r* before the final consonant and the vowel has been been rounded before *r* (compare the development of the vowel in *court* in 1.3). The Gothic noun *huzd* comes to mean *treasure* and appears in *Matthew* 6.21 along with *haírt-ō*, the east Germanic form of the Old English *heort-e* discussed above:

þarei áuk ist **huzd** *izwar, þaruh ist jah haírtō izwar.*
Where then is the **hoard** of you, there is also the *heart* of you.

A suitable *custodian* of your *hoard* may be a guard dog. The origin of the word *dog* is a bit mysterious, but the alternative term *hound* - with a non-original final *d* that may have appeared by association with the final sound of the verb stem *hunt* - is more easily traced. By shifting our *h* back to *k*, we can group the Old English form *hun(d)* with the Greek *kuon (κύων)* and the Latin *can-is* (as in *can-ine*), seen in *1 Kings* 21.23:

canes *comedent Iezabel in agro Iezrahel*
the dogs shall eat Jezebel by the walls of Jezreel

So, if the double negative in Big Mama Thornton's rock and roll classic *You ain't nothing but a hound dog* weren't enough to get the right-thinking rolling their eyes, she's effectively calling someone a *dog dog*! It is the devil's music indeed.

The respelling during the Middle English period of Old English consonant clusters due to changing pronunciation erected a further barrier to linking cognate words. Pronouns such as *hwæt* turned into *what*, concealing the connection the word has with the Latin *quid*. The initial *kw-* sound of the Latin, which adheres to the original Indo-European form, had changed to *hw-* in the Germanic shift. Likewise we see the similarity between *whom* - originally *hwǣm* in Old English and *hwamma* in Gothic - and the equivalent Latin *quem*, and indeed the Sanskrit *kam* (कम्).

The initial consonants *hl-*, rather than inverting as *hw-* did, simplified to *l-* (see 2.6 for *hlāf* and *loaf*). Another example of this is *hlædder* > *ladder*. The root vowel in the Old English noun, *hlǣ-dder*, has morphed from that in the verbal root whence it derives, *hli-nian*, which goes into modern English without the initial *h* as *lea-n*. If we return to the Old English root *hli-* and reverse the effects of the First Germanic

Consonant Shift, we get *kli-*. This is the form of the root in Greek, where the infinitive *klin-ein* (κλίν-ειν) looks virtually identical to its Old English counterpart *hlin-ian* and also means *to lean*. However, the Greeks, resistant to the wheezy ways of the Teutons, kept their guttural *k*, and subsequent Hellenic imports from *kli-* include *clin-ic* and *clim-ax*. In Greek, *klin-e* (κλίν-η) meant *something you lean on* i.e. a *bed*. As physicians often treat people who are in bed, a Greek word for a medic was *klin-ikos* (κλίν-ικος). A *ladder* is *leaned* (or a *hlædder* is *hlinod*), and the equivalent word for *hlæ-dder* in Greek is *klim-ax* (κλῖμ-αξ). This meant, as in English, *something you put against a wall for the purpose of ascent or descent*. Additionally, Greek rhetoric employed this term for a feature of speech that proceeds by degrees from one thing to another, but these days its main use in English is confined to referring to the highest degree of something. Greek also had the form *klim-a* (κλίμ-α), perhaps more recognisable in its genitive singular form *klim-atos*, meaning a *slope*, and by extension a *region* or *zone* of the earth, and the English word *cli-mate* now tends to refer to the weather in a particular region. The Latin form of this root supplies English with words such as *in-cline* (to *lean towards*), *de-cline* (to *lean* or *fall away*) and *re-cline* (to *lean back*).

I (and U)

If *house* and *houses,* why not *mouse* and *mouses*?
(And if *house* and *mouse*, why *soup*?)
And why *fox* and *vixen*?

Otto Jespersen had an ear for English sounds. The work of this pre-eminent Danish scholar in the field of linguistics in the late nineteenth and early twentieth centuries is a rare monument to a rare intellect and spirit. There can have been few greater proponents of the complete superiority of English, which might explain how he sometimes got a bit carried away:

> There is one expression that continually comes to my mind whenever I think of the English language and compare it with others: it seems positively and expressly *masculine*. It is the language of a grown-up man and has very little childish and feminine about it....Just as an English lady will nearly always write in a manner that in any other country would only be found in a man's hand, in the same manner the language is more manly than any other language I know.

If the juxtaposition of the words *childish* and *feminine* are indicative of his views of women it is not surprising that English ladies were wont to write to Otto in a manner that struck him as quite masculine. He goes on to say that the phonetics of English, on which he was doing pioneering work, are what distinguish it from other tongues:

> I select at random, by way of contrast, a passage from the language of Hawaii: 'I kona hiki ana aku ilaila ua hookipa ia mai la oia me ke aloha pumehana loa.' Thus it goes on, no single word ends in a consonant, and a group of two or more consonants is never found. Can anyone be in doubt that...the total impression is childlike and effeminate? You do not expect much energy or vigour in a people speaking such a language; it seems adapted only to inhabitants of sunny regions where the soil requires scarcely any labour on the part

of man to yield him everything he wants.

It is welcome that our philosophy of language has moved on from according people respect based on the intensity of their consonant clusters, even if that means we are no longer able in polite conversation to talk of Hawaiian as a girly language spoken by people who laze around all day waiting for coconuts to fall on their heads. But for Jespersen and his ilk the sewing together of phonemes produced symphonies, not merely words. So if he occasionally lifted his head and said something a bit wacky, people probably just smiled and said, "Dear old Otto, going on again about how the Hawaiians have a rubbish word for *spoon*." Here is Franz Bopp, Professor of Sanskrit and Comparative Grammar at Berlin in the electrifying days of the early nineteenth century when philological research was racing into new territories, animadverting that long vowels at the end of feminine words are rather smouldering;

> The feminine in Sanscrit, both in the base and in the case-terminations, loves a luxurious fullness of form; and where it is distinguished from the other genders in the base or in the termination, it marks this distinction by broader, and more sonant vowels. The neuter, on the other hand, prefers the greatest conciseness.

I wonder if he wrote that after his intense concentration had been interrupted, if only *für einen Augenblick*, by the sight of a fruity *Fräulein* floating fragrantly past his open window. It is also telling that he uses the word *conciseness* with its connotations of cutting in relation to the neuter form. One almost expects him to talk of the masculine as upright or prominent. And this is just grammar - Bopp on vocabulary is positively lewd.

Among Jespersen's achievements was his work on what he called the Great Vowel Shift, that sequence of sound changes whose effects were extreme - it is the main feature distinguishing the phonologies of Middle English and Modern English. An example is the change in the word for a small rodent often chased by cats, which went from *mūs* (pronounced *moose*) to *mouse* (pronounced like *house*). What occupied Jespersen primarily was sound, but there is clearly a major issue with spelling here too. The respelling of *mūs* as *mouse* was a French idea which preceded by some time the actual change in pronunciation. After a considerable influx of foreign vocabulary with its own spelling conventions, spelling variations reflecting either dialectical differences or scribal preferences multiplied during the Middle English period. With the sound changes wrought by the Great Vowel Shift as well, some of the most vital elements of English spelling had gone totally haywire by the time of Shakespeare. Consequently, spelling is one of the most fundamentally problematic areas of English.

A sound grounding in Old English phonetics allows a novice to predict the pronunciation of an Old English word within a fairly narrow range (notwithstanding the impossibility of precisely pinning down all the sounds of a dead language). The range of vowels was smaller then than now. Accurate prediction is far more complex in the modern language, especially with vowels. For example, in *mouse* (< *mūs*), *house* (< *hūs*) and *mouth* (< *mūþ* as in 1.1) the letters *ou* represent a diphthongal modification of the original simple vowel *ū*   (i.e. it becomes the vowels *a* and *u* in succession), but in *soup* (< *sūp*) they represent the original *ū*.

The diphthongisation of the *ū* of *mūs*, *hūs* and *mūþ* occurred in the Great Vowel Shift. It was blocked, however, by certain nearby sounds which – like *oo* – were also produced using the lips, such as the following labial consonant *p* in *soup*. So, before a meal we ask for something that sounds like *soop* and not *sowp* or *saup*. Diphthongisation was also blocked by the preceding labial *w*, which is why the vowel in *wound* (meaning *injury*) sounds the same as that in *soup*. (The past tense of the verb *wind* – also *wound* and therefore theoretically also immune to diphthongisation – has nevertheless changed by analogy with *find* and *found* which belonged to the same class in Old English). Diphthongisation also did not happen before *r* + consonant, which is why we say *court* the way we do. But *r* + consonant did not just block one change, it caused another. The vowel in *court* is not pronounced like the vowel in *soup* because the following *rt* lowered the vowel to an *or* sound (compare Gothic *huzd* and Old English *hord* in 1.2). The problem, then, is not really the sounds themselves, which behave according to highly regular patterns, but the way those sounds are represented in spelling. First the spelling of the original sound changed, then the pronunciation of the sound itself changed while the spelling remained static. The problem seen here of predicting pronunciation points to another problem, of predicting plural forms. Why *mouse* and *mice*, but *house* and *houses*?

Many letters now redundant to pronunciation are retained. You could argue - and spelling reformists like George Bernard Shaw would have - that at least two letters from the sexiliteral *taught* could be eliminated, particularly as the quadriliteral words *tort* and *taut* share its pronunciation. On the other hand the sound which explains some of the most fascinating features of English, though itself redundant for at least two thousand years, is rarely still present in spelling to unlock the supremely logical pattern in words such as *mouse* and *mice*. The Old English singular was *mūs* and the plural *mȳs* - the difference in sound being that *ū* is a back vowel and *ȳ* a front vowel, which terms refer to the part of the tongue used in producing the sound. The difference was slight but decisive because these front and back vowels then developed independently into the modern sounds in *mouse* and *mice*. But why was there a different vowel in the first place?

Before any Old English was recorded the plural form of *mūs* was not *mȳs* but **mūs-i*. The *i* plural marker is a front vowel and it came to influence the pronunciation of the preceding back vowel *ū*, moving its place of articulation further and further forward until it become *ȳ*. Then the final *i* faded away to leave *mȳs*. The same process accounts for the Gothic verb *huzd-jan* and its Old English equivalent *hyd-an* (see 1.2) > *hide*. The sequence is thus:

*mūs-i > *mȳs-i > mȳs > mice

However, the plural of *house* is not *hice*. The above process did not occur with Old English *hūs*. Whereas *mūs* was a feminine noun, *hūs* was neuter. The form of a neuter noun was the same in both the singular and plural of the nominative case. So the *i* plural marker did not occur, the root vowel was unaffected, and later the default plural marker *s* was adopted in conformity with most nouns.

There are instances where this infectious *i* has not been entirely excised. Take the reconstructed form **fuhs-in*. As with *mūs-i*, the back vowel *u* is changed to *y* by the following front vowel *i*. The medial *hs* then becomes *ks*, shortened to *x*:

*fuhs-in > *fyhs-in > *fyx-in > vix-en

Not subject to i-umlaut the counterpart **fuhs-a* develops differently. As well as vowels being classified back and front, such as *ū* and *ȳ*, they are also classified high, middle, or low. Back vowels can thus be placed on a vertical scale:

u

o

a

A tendency to harmonise vowels caused the high vowel *u* to be low-

29

ered when the following syllable contained a non-high vowel. Thus the final low vowel *a* turned **fuhs-a* into **fohs-a*. (Similarly accounted for is *daught-er*, appearing in Old English as *doht-or* where an original *u* as found in the Sanskrit *duhit-ṛ* (दुहितृ) and Greek *thugat-ēr* (θυγάτ-ηρ) is lowered to *o* by a following non-high vowel.) The final unstressed vowel *a* then dropped off (like the *i* of **mūs-i*) to leave **fohs*:

*fuhs-a > *fohs-a > *fohs > fox

The initial *f*/*v* alternation is a muddle of Middle English dialects. The forms *vox* and *fixen* also occurred alongside the *fox* and *vixen* before the modern forms were settled on.

Mostly though, after *i* had done its thing and been absorbed into preceding sounds it disappeared from view. This is a sort of diachronic version of the process observed by the fourth century B.C. Sanskrit grammarian Pāṇini in his *Aṣṭādhyāyī*. Rule 1.1.62 states:

प्रत्ययलोपे   प्रत्ययलक्षणम्
pratyayalope   *pratyayalakṣaṇam*

(where there is) affix elision (there remains the) affix mark

This means that when an affix (for example the *i* of **mūs-i*) has been elided, an operation directed by that affix is still effective. In other words, the *i* affix causes the vowel change distinguishing *mȳs* from *mūs* despite itself later being elided. i.e. the form is *mȳs* not **mȳs-i*. This process has been referred to as rephonologization. Elsewhere, with reference to the Tibeto-Burman language Lahu, James Madisoff has called it Cheshirization. At one point in *Alice's Adventures in Wonderland*, the Cheshire cat gradually disappears until only its famous grin is left behind.

The presence and role of *i* were further obscured by the orthographic chaos that followed the Great Vowel Shift. Still its mark is everywhere, and to check we can trace many words into Gothic which retained it and where it did not infect the preceding vowel. It is represented as *j* (and pronounced *y*) before a vowel. For example, Old English has the noun *fōd-a*, meaning *food*, and the same word in Gothic is *fōd-eins*. The original root vowel *ō* is retained in the English because there is no *i*/*j* in the following syllable to change it. The Gothic verb, however, is *fod-jan*, and in the pre-textual period of Old English that *j* fronted the vowel

30

in the Old English verb to *fēd-an* before itself disappearing. We are left with two words, the noun *food* and the verb *feed*, and no obvious clue as to the cause of the variation.

This process, discovered by the great German philologist and famous teller of fairy tales Jakob Grimm, is called i-mutation or i-umlaut. It is the string by which we trace our way out of the labyrinth which has grown up around our language as century has followed century, and it leads us to a plateau from which we see no longer the modern jumbling juggernaut that sprawls over the entire world, but a tight bud reaching up from the misty forests of northern Europe at the dawn of English culture, only just beginning to stretch away from its roots. So put that in your peep and smack it, as somebody in fifteenth century England is unlikely to have said.

1.4

Ablaut and Umlaut

Why are there irregular verbs? And if *teach*, why *taught*?

Modern English is said to have regular verbs and irregular verbs. This is based on the observation that in the past tense most end in *–ed* (*studied*, *work-ed*) while a few do not (*rode*, *cut*). That the latter number so few against the size of the default *–ed* group heightens their exoticism, and their variety of forms certainly seems to justify the classification as irregular. They appear to have little in common with the default class and sometimes even less in common with each other. However, changes in sound and spelling have obfuscated matters here as they did in relation to i-umlaut (see 1.3). In fact most English irregular verbs are not irregular at all from a historical point of view. They are relics of Old English strong verbs whose conjugations follow a strict system of vowel gradation or ablaut - *drive, drove, driv-en* < *drīf-e, drāf, drif-en* shares its pattern with *ride, rode, ridd-en* < *rīd-e, rād, rid-en*. The vowel sounds here have barely changed in more than fifteen hundred years, but these are exceptionally resilient examples. What we see in the current state of the English irregular class is a terminal stage in the disintegration of one of the most archaic, beautiful and pervasive features of Indo-European languages.

The Victorian philologist Joseph Wright wrote that, "...although the series of vowels is seen most clearly in the stem-forms of strong verbs, the learner must not assume that ablaut occurs in strong verbs only. Every *syllable* of every word of whatever part of speech contains some form of ablaut." Elsewhere the French linguist Antoine Meillet stated that, "The only stable constituent portion of an Indo-European morphological element is the consonantal portion. The vocalic portion is always subject to alternation." If we took the term "Indo-European" out, Meillet's description would seem to the casual observer more apt for describing something like Arabic's tri-consonantal root system than something like English. The great Sanskrit grammarian Pāṇini, led the way. (It took the Europeans another two thousand years to figure this stuff out, which they did just as they started learning Sanskrit.) He even refers to vowel gradation at the very beginning of his opus. Sanskrit vowels are arranged on a scale whose highest grade is called *vṛddhi* (वृद्धि). This word comes from a verbal root meaning *grow*. Growth is a positive thing, and Sanskrit texts conventionally have as their first word something benedictive. Hence *vṛddhi* is the very first word of Pāṇini's very first sutra *vṛddhirādaic* (वृद्धिरादैच्), which states that the term denotes the sounds *ā*, *ai* and *au*. That's how important vowel gradation is. Yet the handful of English verbs displaying vestiges of this marvellous system are these days referred to almost pejoratively as irregular. To understand its presence in English we first need to know what it is and why it existed in the first place.

As the surviving irregular verbs are faded, wind-scattered embers of a mighty linguistic explosion, so the morphological complexity of classical languages such as Sanskrit and Ancient Greek is a snapshot of that explosion at the peak of its radiative force. At this point each form is on a clear and linear trajectory so we can easily see where it came from. Then the momentum runs out and things begin to drift. We shall return to this early stage of decay shortly. The moments after the initial blast saw the first divergences from Proto-Indo-European sounds occurring as speakers began to migrate in different directions away from their homeland. Before the fuse was lit, things seem to have been pretty simple.

Virtually all Proto-Indo-European verbal roots contained non-high vowels, by far the commonest of which was **e*. Depending on where the accent fell on a word this default sound alternated with either **o* or nothing (which can be represented as ϕ). Hence words are said to be based on either e-grade, o-grade or ϕ-grade (zero-grade) forms of the root. This pattern can clearly be seen in three Greek words derived from the root **pet* meaning *fly*, where accented vowels are indicated:

e-grade	o-grade	ϕ-grade
πέτ-ομαι	ποτ-ανός	ἐ-πτ-όμην
pét-omai	pot-anós	e-pt-ómēn
I fly	winged (adj.)	I flew

A non-Hellenist could now recognise the zero-grade of this root in the name of the winged reptile the *pt-ero-dactyl*, and also *helico-pt-er* (see 1.5 for more on *helix*). This is about as simple as it gets. If we try to find the same kind of pattern in ancient Germanic languages we see that other factors have already begun to obscure the original vowel sequence. Drift has set in. Three principle parts of the verb *help* in Gothic are:

e-grade	o-grade	ø-grade
hilp-an	*halp*	*hulp-um*
to help	*I helped*	*we helped*

Here the original **e > i* and original *o > a*. Most interesting is what has happened to the zero-grade form where we would expect to see the root with no vowel. In Modern English the nucleus of every syllable must be a vowel sound e.g. h*e*lp, h*e*lp*e*r, *u*nh*e*lpf*u*l, and the sound *l* is generally treated as a consonant. In Proto-Indo-European *l* could also serve as a syllabic nucleus (which it does to some extent in English words like ab*l*e). This meant that before Gothic *hulp-um* there would have been a form like **hlp-um*. Germanic fully vocalised *l* in this position so it developed into *ul*. The corresponding forms in Old English are:

e-grade	o-grade	ø-grade
help-an	*healp*	*hulp-on < *hlp-on*

Here the Gothic o-grade form *halp* has been further changed before *l* to *ea* in a process known as breaking and explored further in 1.5 (although resistance to breaking in the West Saxon dialect preserved *e* in the infinitive).

In summary, strong verbs thus have ablaut patterns originally determined by the movement of the accent around Proto-Indo-European roots. Surrounding sounds such as *l* subsequently caused further changes to certain vowels and these were responsible for Old English strong verbs splintering into seven classes. At this point, the ablaut system in English seems to have reached a limit of complexity and the momentum from the original explosion completely ran out. Some strong verbs drifted across to the weak conjugation. Our example *help* had an Old English past participle *holp-en* according to the class three pattern also seen in *melt / molt-en* and *swell / swoll-en*. Only *swollen* remains as a common participle, while *molten* has a restricted use and all three of those verbs now have weak preterites ending in *–ed*. Some strong verbs disappeared altogether, although many survive in other Germanic languages.

In both Germanic and Romance languages the reaction against complex systems of ablaut seems to have had far-reaching consequences. English is very unusual in preserving the preterite or past simple e.g. *I helped* as a major feature of verbal conjugation alongside a periphrastic perfect *I have helped*. The latter has a rather peculiar meaning not discretely expressed by equivalent forms in other languages. While English has standardised nearly all past simples to the –ed group, in other languages the default form corresponding in meaning to the English past simple is the periphrastic perfect using an auxiliary verb. In German the periphrastic *ich habe geholfen* is more widely used than *ich half* to mean *I helped*. The French one-word preterite is eclipsed in frequency by constructions using *have* or *be* auxiliary verbs + past participle e.g. *j'ai aidé*.

In addition to the surviving strong verbs of Old English, there are also a good number of verbs classified irregular in Modern English which are not even strong verbs. They form their past tenses entirely regularly with what is almost universally represented nowadays as -ed, but variously pronounced –d as in *roll-ed*, -t as in *walk-ed*, or -id as in *want-ed*. These are the weak verbs of Old English. They are not subject to vowel gradation, and in the past tense they all end in one of the sounds generated by the suffix represented as -ed. An example of a weak verb in Old English that makes it onto the list of regular verbs in Modern English is *love* with a past tense *loved* which has an easily identifiable tense suffix. Focus on the sound and not the spelling, and you see that *send*, with its past tense *sent* is also one of these. It may not be spelt with the regular -ed ending, but it ends with the same sound as *walk-ed*, and no there is no change of vowel. All that has happened is the weak ending has been efficiently absorbed into the homogeneous final consonant. It is certainly a long way from *drink, drank, drunk*.

The third group of verbs that are lumped in as irregular are ones which, like *send*, are entirely regular in taking the weak -ed type ending, but which have undergone a change of root vowel not accountable for by the Indo-European ablaut sequences. That is to say that verbs like *teach* and *buy* with their past participles *taught* and *bought* do not fit in any of the seven classes of vowel gradation to which belong verbs such as *drive* and *see*. The apparent irregularity is again due to an entirely regular sequence of changes, and this time the changes are driven by i-umlaut.

The Germanic verbal root for *teach* was *tak*. The infinitive, which formed the basis of the present stem was *tak-jan*. When it went into English the voiced palatal *j* merged with the unvoiced stem-final velar *k* to make the unvoiced palatal *ch* sound (represented in Old English as *c*) and producing *tacan* (see 1.6 for the same process in Sanskrit). But, as the *i* of *mūs-i* fronted its *ū* into the *ȳ* of *mȳs*, so *j* of *tak-jan* also fronted the root vowel *a* to *æ* to produce the actual infinitive *tæc-an* whose vowel was later raised to the *ee* sound of *teach*:

*tak-jan > tǣc-an > teach

The past tense, however, did not share the *-jan* suffix of the infinitive. It used the suffix *–de* (known in Modern English as *–ed*). So i-umlaut did not occur, the root vowel was unchanged, the palatalisation of *k* was blocked, the stem remained *tak-*, and the voiceless stem-final *k* devoiced the consonant in the suffix to turn *de* into *te*.. The *k* of *tak-te* then became *h* (see 1.2) by the First Germanic Consonant Shift giving the past tense *tāhte* (although the West Saxon dialect's *tǣh-te*, with umlauted vowel analogous with the present, is anomalous). From here the vowel was rounded (as in *gans* and *gōs*, see 1.1) and it was a small step to the pronunciation used now for *taught*:

*tak-te > tāh-te > taugh-t

The last of the irregulars are such as *can* and *will* (see 4.3), and the ultimate non-conformer *be* (see 2.2).

1.5

More I and H

If *teach* and *taught*, why *buy* and *bought*, and *think* and *thought*? Why does *brung* sound okay but *thunk* sound silly? And if *see*, why *saw*?

In 1.2 we saw the interchange of *k* and *h* at the start of words, so the Latin *cord-* corresponds to the Sanskrit *hṛd* found in the eastern reaches of Indo-European and to the English *heart* in the westernmost. Sanskrit sometimes retains *k*, as in the word for *night*, which is *nakt-* (नक्त्). We can compare Latin *noct-*, Greek *nukt-* (νυκτ-), German *nacht*, Gothic *naht-*, Old English *niht*.) In Sanskrit this *k* alternates with *sh*, so the number 8 is *aṣṭa* (अष्ट pronounced like *ashta*) against the Greek *oktō* (ὀκτώ). Germanic languages developed a sound somewhere between *k* and *sh*. The German for *8* is *acht*, which retains a sound similar to the hard *xh* - written *h* - of Gothic *ahtáu* and Old English *eahta*. (Contrast the development of this sound in the initial position of words like *heart*, where it has softened to a mere aspiration and is often dropped altogether in certain dialects.) For simplicity's sake, in the following section the letter *h* is to be taken as a hard *xh* unless otherwise stated. This sound is one of the chief havoc-mongers in the history of English, responsible for some fundamental changes in pronunciation. These decisively differentiated English from its continental Germanic relatives and led to the superficially inexplicable pairings and misleading similarities listed in the title of this section.

Eahta is a simple example. What distinguishes it from the Gothic and the German is that the initial vowel sound *a* (the Germanic development of an original *o* as preserved in Greek *oktō*) has become the diphthong *ea* by a process known as breaking (seen in 1.4 where Gothic *halp* contrasts with Old English *healp*). This occurred when front vowels such as *a* were immediately followed by one or more velar or velarised consonants such as *h*.

If *aht-* becomes *eaht-* as the stem of the Old English number 8, why then does *naht-* not yield **neaht-* as the stem for the Old English word for *night*, rather than the form *niht-* cited above, and why do we not

37

now pronounce it as *neight to rhyme with eight? Briefly, the original a was indeed diphthongised (*neaht), but where the final sound of eaht-a is the low vowel a (see 1.3) the Proto-Germanic form of *neaht had an ending with the high vowel i. This caused i-umlaut (see 1.3) of the diphthong ea, raising and re-monophthongising it to e to form neht. The subsequent palatalisation of h before t produced a sh sound (*neçt, still spelt with h) formed at the top of the mouth which further raised e to i (*niçt) in a process of palatal umlaut. The subsequent elision of the sound sh in Middle English lengthened the i to a long ee sound (*neet) which was re-diphthongised in the Great Vowel Shift to become what we have in our word night. In brief, the original short vowel was diph-thongised, re-monophthongised, and then re-diphthongised again in the sequence:

*nokt > *nakt > *naht > *neaht > neht > niht > night

Each of these stages occurred because of the h which followed it – firstly because the h was there, then because it changed, then because it faded away.

Following the same route was Old English lēoht (lēht in the Old Mercian dialect) > light. Here, as with night and noct- etc., the conti-nental languages better preserved the original velar sound k. Hence Lat-in lux (< *luc-s) > Luc-ifer, lumen (< *luc-men) > il-lumin-ate, and Greek leuk-os (λευκ-ός) > leukaemia.

In addition to the effect of h on preceding vowels, the other main consideration in explaining the forms in this section's title is suffixa-tion. In 1.3 we saw the phenomenon of i-umlaut. This explains how the infinitival suffix –jan followed the Germanic root tak (teach) producing the Old English infinitive by the sequence *takjan > tǣcan, and leading to teach. The past tense suffix –te on the same root produced the preterite by *tak-te > tāh-te, leading to taught. Different suffixes for the infinitive and the preterite caused different developments in the root.

By the Middle English period the sound h itself had become quite unstable when initial in a medial or final consonant cluster, as evi-denced by a range of spellings which began to favour a preceding g. Over time what appears in modern spelling as gh at the end of a sylla-ble or before t was either eliminated from pronunciation altogether (night and taught) or became the f sound heard in tough. This was not a simple step, it depended on the vowel which preceded it, and there was clearly dialectical variation. There are examples of seventeenth and eighteenth century writers rhyming after and daughter, and in some cases spelling the latter dafter. The same goes for several of these gh and *ght* words in that period. But this was the last and least important change in a sequence that had involved some of the most interesting processes in the history and prehistory of English.

Evolving similarly to *teach/taught* are *buy/bought*. Gothic confirms that the original form of *buy* was *bug* and it took the common infinitival suffix *–jan* to make *bugjan*. The English and the Gothic diverged from each other in the infinitive due to i-umlaut, which operated exclusively on English. In English the *j* element began its slow transformation of the word, palatalising the preceding *g* (like **tak-jan* becoming **tac-an*, see 1.3) to produce **bucg-an* - in which the *cg* cluster sounded like *dge* in *bri-dge* - and mutating the root vowel to make the actual Old English form *bycg-an*. (Compare this *u/y* alternation with the singular/plural vowel alternation of *mūs/mȳs* in 1.3.) Meanwhile none of this had happened in Gothic, which thus retained the more original *bug-jan*.

Even before i-umlaut though, the Germanic preterite had diverged from the infinitive. The past tense marker *–te* (*ta* in Gothic) on **bug-te* (Gothic **bug-ta*) devoiced *g* to *k* producing **buk-te* (**buk-ta*). As in Greek *oktō* and Old English *eahta* the original *k* became Germanic *h* to produce **buh-te* (**buh-ta*). Then the root vowel was lowered by influence of the vowel in the preterite suffix to give the actual Old English *boh-te* and Gothic *baúh-ta*. When the unstressed final vowel faded away we were left with basically what we have in Modern English – *bough-t*. The i-umlauted infinitive *bycg-an* also lost its final syllable and was put through the Middle English spelling mangle, emerging as the frenchified *buy* (again compare the sound change in *mȳs* becoming *mice*). So:

bug-jan > *bucg-an > bycg-an > *bycg > buy

*bug-te > *buk-te > *buh-te > boh-te > bough-t

Incorporating an additional strand of change are *think* and *thought*. Again we can start by comparing the Gothic infinitive *þagk-jan* (where the *gk* sequence represents a sound like the *nk* in *think*) and the Old English infinitive *þenc-an*, where i-umlaut had raised the root vowel from original *a* (and *c* coming after *n* was a hard *k* and not the palatal *ch* of *tǽcan*). In the preterite the original *a* of the root was lengthened (and in Old English rounded) as the final *k* became *h* giving Old English *þōh-te* and Gothic *þāh-ta*. That's very nice, but a question remains. Where did the *n* go? In 1.1 we saw how the languages in the Ingvaeonic subgroup disposed of *n* before certain spirants (or fricatives) and lengthened a preceding vowel, which accounts for English *mouth* against German *Munt*. A similar change had occurred prior to that across the Germanic languages when *n* was followed by *h* (which, don't forget, in our historical context was a fricative *xh* sound). So, before *þōh-te* we assume a form with a nasal like **þanh-te*. The same goes for *bring* and *brought*. However, an important difference exists between *think* and *bring*.

There is a low budget form of motorsport in which you take whatever car you like – the company van, your granny's hatchback, a rental car, or even a full-spec competition car – to a dragster racing venue and blast it up the quarter mile strip as many times as you want until it falls to bits. It's not a race, you don't need a licence, and hardly anybody comes to watch. It is known as *Run What Ya Brung*. (The name is too fossilised now to lobby for a change to *Run What You Have Brought*.) Most English speakers would probably admit to at least a vague intuitive awareness that *brung* is somehow a logical alternative to - albeit a poor relation of – *brought*. But tell someone, "I thunk about you all night" and they will suspect you of playing some hilarious lexical prank. Or, to put it another way, if Old English *þōh-te* (*thought*) goes with an infinitive *þenc-an*, why does Old English *brōh-te* (*brought*) not have an infinitive *breng-an*? Its actual infinitive is *bring-an*, in the vast majority of cases.

These two verbs, like *teach* and *buy*, were weak in Old English, which is to say they formed their preterites using the *-te* type suffix corresponding to modern *–ed*, hence *þōh-te* and *brōh-te*. But while *þenc-an* was always clearly a weak verb, *bring-an* looks like it could be a class three strong verb like *sing/sang/sung* and *begin/began/begun*. Was it originally a weak verb reformulated by analogy with class three strong verbs? This is unlikely given that the move from weak to strong is very rare – the travel is overwhelmingly in the other direction. Was it then a class three strong verb which drifted into the weak conjugation, adopting the weak preterite suffix to make *brōh-te* but retaining its original vowel in the infinitive *bring-an*? In support of this there are some examples of a strong past participle *brung-en* in Old English. Against it we find that the strong preterite *brang* seems to have been only a dialectical mutant, the weak preterite *brōh-te* is far more prevalent, and there is occasionally found a characteristically weak infinitive *breng-an*. This seems to leave us at something of an impasse.

What we have here is a hybrid. While the present tense of *bring-an* had the syllable structure of a class three strong verb like *sing-an*, it originally had a weak preterite like *þōh-te*. The strong present encouraged the use of ablaut and led to non-standard forms like *brung*, while the weak preterite caused occasional reformulation of the infinitive as the weak *bring-an*. Neither innovation stuck, and this remarkable fossil from Proto-Germanic remains virtually intact. Straddling the strong and weak categories *bring* has a residual ambiguity which allows for *brung*, while we would not *think* of saying *thunk*.

Firmly in the strong category, historically and still now, is *see*. In Old English this belonged to class five. A more typical member of this class was the ancestor of *speak* (whose vowels followed a pattern of infinitive *sprec-an*, present *spric-*, preterite singular *spræc*, preterite plural *spræc-on*, past participle *sprec-en*, which have become the simpler *speak*, *spoke*, *spok-en* of the contemporary language). But *see* was the nexus of several processes – the First Germanic Consonant Shift, the Second Germanic Consonant Shift, i-umlaut, intervocalic consonant elision, syncopation of unstressed vowels, and dialect-specific pre-velar diphthongisation - which, by the Old English period, had produced a magnificently eccentric conjugation that takes a bit of untangling and seems disproportionately complex for such a short word. In respect of form it has a strong case for being quite the most interesting verb in English.

See derives from a Proto-Indo-European form *sek^w*, whose sense of *follow* is reflected in the Latin *sequ-or* (whence *sequ-ence*) and the Greek *hép-omai* (ἕπ-ομαι – see 1.6 for development of Greek labials such as *p* from original velars such as *k*). From this root we can see how the First Germanic Consonant Shift changed *k* to *h* to produce a Germanic *sehw-* which went into Gothic as *saíƕ-an* (where *ƕ=hw*). The pre-velar diphthongisation which made the *a* in Gothic *ahtáu* into the *ea* of Old English *eahta* made the *e* of *sehw-* (represented in Gothic spelling as the *aí* of the infinitive *saíƕ-an*) into *eo* in a Proto-Old-English infinitive *seohw-an*. The same process broke the vowel in the first singular preterite from the Gothic *saƕ* to Old English *seah*. But while the final *h* of the Old English preterite *seah* was preserved, the intervocalic *h* of the infinitive was lost producing *sēo-an* which then contracted to *sēon*. By contrast the intervocalic *ƕ* in Gothic *saíƕ-an* was not lost, and it remains in the Modern German infinitive *seh-en*. The absence of *h* and the presence of the long diphthong in the Old English infinitive *sēon* are also features of the first person singular present *sēo* (*I see*). If *h* is dropped only when intervocalic we must assume that that this form originally ended with *h* + a vowel, which derived from the original *w* of *sehw-*. That vowel itself disappeared once it had contributed to the loss of *h*. So in all these three Old English forms – the infinitive, the first singular present, and the first singular preterite - there is initially breaking of the root vowel before *h*:

Infinitive
*sehw-an   >   *seohw-an

First singular present
*sehw   >   *seohu

First singular preterite
*sah   >   seah

While the preterite settled with this form the other two then underwent loss of *h* and contraction of the remaining vowels:

Infinitive
*sehw-an   >   *seohw-an   >   *sēo-an   >   sēo-n

First singular present
*sehw   >   *seohu   >   *sēou   >   sēo

Given that the second person singular present *you see* in Gothic is *saíhv-is*, where the *h* is clearly intervocalic (between the root vowel and the *i* of the termination *–is*) we would expect the Old English to have dropped it. Instead we have *sih-st*, where not only is the *h* retained but the root vowel has changed. Again we have a case of i-umlaut. From a basic form *seh-ist*, the vowel of the ending *–ist* raised the root vowel from *e* to *i* producing *sih-ist*. Then the unstressed umlaut-triggering *i* vowel of the termination was subject to syncope i.e. it dropped out to leave *sih-st*, (compare the Modern German *sieh-st*) where the *h* is no longer intervocalic. This syncope process must therefore have happened in an earlier period *before* the process of loss of intervocalic *h*, otherwise the form would be something like *si-st*. The sequence is:

*seh-ist   >   *sih-ist   >   *sih-st

In the preterite, however, there is yet more going on. In the preterite the root vowel of class three verbs in Old English changes to *æ* in the singular and *ǣ* in the plural, giving as a model *spræc* (*I spoke*) and *sprǣc-on* (*we spoke*). The *h* of the *see* verb breaks the vowel *æ* to produce *seah* in the singular for *I saw*. But the Modern English form *saw* looks far more like the second person singular *sāw-e* or the plural forms *sāw-on*, and how did we get there from an infinitive *sēon*?

The *w* of *sāw-e* is a vestige of the original *h*. Although it was inter-

42

vocalic and should have been subject to elision, here it was preserved by the Second Germanic Consonant Shift, which accounts for some crucial differences between English and German. We have seen how the First Germanic Consonant Shift changed the original *k* of Indo-European to *xh* in Germanic (which has been appearing as *h* in our spellings) which differentiates Latin *sequ-* and Gothic *saíƕ-*. We have seen how this sound was elided in the Old English infinitive to turn *seoh-an* into *sēon*. Before this elision could happen in the preterite where *h* would have been intervocalic between the root vowel and the vowel of the termination, the Second Germanic Consonant Shift changed the voiceless *xh* of *saxh-* into a voiced form which we might represent as *sagh-*. This happened because in the preterite the stress of *sāw-e* originally fell on the ending. (In the infinitive *seoh-an* the stress originally fell on the root. The voicing process cannot occur if the immediately preceding syllable is stressed. See 2.2. and 2.4 for more on this.) This voiced *gh* then became a *g* in Anglian dialects and a *w* in West Saxon, neither of which was subject to intervocalic elision. The sequence is:

*sak > *saxh > *sagh > sag / saw

The other feature which distinguishes this form from the first person singular is the vowel. The *h* breaks the root vowel *æ* to make *seah* (*I saw*), compared to the unbroken class three form *spræc* (*I spoke*). The *w* (formerly break-triggering *h*) blocks this. Further, there are several attested forms of these words, so as well as *sāw-* there is also *saw-*. The Anglian preference for *g* over *w* gives us *sæg-on*, which brings us back to where we started in this section with the number 8. The *æ* of *sæg-on* is a long form of the *a* (strictly *æ*) in *aht-* which becomes *eaht-* in Old English because of the following *h*. The *g* of *sæg-on* is a velar like *h* – and as we have seen was originally *h* – so we might expect a form *seag-on* to match the singular *seah*. But pre-velar diphthongisation was blocked by the voicing of *g*, so the root vowel remains unbroken.

At the end of this remarkably intricate process we have *see* and *saw*.

1.6

K and G

How *quick*, *vivacious* and *antibiotic* are related.

Hail native Language, that by sinews weak
   Didst move my first endeavouring tongue to speak,
   And madst imperfect words with childish tripps,
   Half unpronounc't, slide through my infant-lipps,
   Driving dum silence from the portal dore
   Where he had mutely sate two years before.

Thus Milton addresses language, and one imagines that language would be rather impressed. By contrast, when Shakespeare has the Earl of Kent rant, "Thou whoreson zed! thou unnecessary letter", in King Lear, one imagines that alphabetic terminus feeling quite hurt. Milton's "half unpronounc't" and "imperfect words" put me in mind of my own early struggles to get sounds in the right order. I said *par cark* for *car park*, and *ambliance* for *ambulance*. Sounds can easily be jumbled up or misrecognised. Arabic uses the sound *b* but not *p*, and it can be difficult for Arabic speakers to hear the difference between the two in English. This explains how an acquaintance of mine dining in a seafood restaurant in Kuwait was offered roasted crap (at least I think it does). Japanese speakers sometimes conflate *r* and *l*. The two are not precisely homogeneous sounds, but almost. They are produced in the same area of the mouth by the same organs. A confused Japanese would not be enlightened by listening to the neo-Received Pronunciation of some BBC radio announcers, who also mix the two sounds. Words with an intervocalic *r* like *parade* come out as *palade*. That's not how the Queen says it.
   Sound change normally has more interesting and systematic causes than just being a narcissistic middle-class weirdo. For example, superficially there is nothing to connect the English word *tear* - sad eye water - with the French word *larme*, which also means *tear*. Historically, though, they are the same word. The English is related to a Germanic form found in Gothic as *tagr*, and the French to the Latin *lacr-i-ma* - in both the guttural consonant has been worn away through time and the

words passed through intermediate forms, *ta(g)r* and *la(c)r(i)ma*. The crucial thing here is that the Latin word was not originally *lacr-i-ma* but *dacr-i-ma*. This can be cross-referenced with the Greek *dakr-u* (δάκϱ-υ.) The First Germanic Consonant Shift changed the *d* of *dakr-u* to *t* in *tagr*. Latin turned *d* to *l* and added a suffix *-ma*, but we are dealing with the same word here.

The relationship between *quick* and *bio-* has similarly been buried under a mound of splintered sounds. First, let us assume a proto-form **gwiw-os*, which does not occur in any recorded language but which is broadly reconstructable by working backward through processes of sound change in different branches of Indo-European. The First Germanic Consonant Shift tells us that *g* goes to *k* in Germanic (also see 2.6), giving us **kwiw-os*. From this Gothic derives the adjective *qius* (from a stem *qiw-*) meaning *alive* and allied to a verb *ga-qiu-nan*, to *be made alive*. Gothic *q* is transcribed in English as *c*, so the equivalent adjective in Old English was *cwi-c*. These days, the word has a more Gothic look about it after the Normans independently fiddled around with the spelling and made it *qui-ck*. Although it now means *speedy*, in Old English *cwic* meant *alive* (hence "the *quick* and the dead", coined in the King James Bible). While the mead quaffers of the North Sea littoral hacked away at **gwiw-os* with their cackling gutturals, the olive squeezers of southern Europe favoured the *-w-*of the initial consonant cluster and dropped the *g* altogether. So, **gwiw-os* went into Latin as *viv-us*, where the *v* represents the sound *w*. Allied to this form of the adjective is the verb *viv-ere*, to *live*. The French word for *meat* is *viande*, which is a simplification of the Latin gerundive *viv-enda*, meaning *things to be lived on*. From this root English has words such as *revive* and *viv-acious*.

A little earlier I mentioned the easy conflation of *r* and *l* by Japanese speakers, owing to the similarities in their places and organs of generation. (The reference here is to the sounds *r* and *l*'s organs of generation. The location of Japanese people's organs of generation is not relevant here.) Speakers of some South Asian languages have a similar problem with *b* and *v*. Close your lips slightly when saying the sound *v* and you will see how easy it is, especially for a speaker of a language which does not make that distinction. Once in Saudi Arabia, I was baffled by an incident involving the unvoiced forms *p* and *f*. I was accosted outside a barber's shop by a Philippina woman who said, to my surprise, "I give you pliers, I give you pliers!" I replied that although it may seem to her that I needed pliers, that was in fact not the case. Nevertheless she rushed off and back with a handful of leaflets and said, "Pliers for my shop!" A similar thing must have happened with the Greeks and

45

gwiwos, even though they did originally have a *w* sound. As in Latin, the *g* disappears, but in Greek it seems to have been absorbed by the *w* which turned into *b*, and gradually the second *w* is lost to make *bios*. (See 2.11 for the similar case of Latin *glan-s* and Greek *balan-os*.) As a result, the Latin *vi-ta* meaning *life* and yielding words such as *vi-tal*, is basically the same as the Greek *bio-te (βιοτή)* whence *anti-bio-tic*, *pro-bio-tic* and so forth.

Sanskrit, however, kept the *g*. Let us assume a form *giw*. But I hear you all cry, "That is no Sanskrit root known to us!" And you are quite right. We have seen elsewhere that vowels can be classified as front or back according to where they are generated in the mouth. We can also locate them more specifically. For example, *i* is a palatal vowel. As the term suggests, the palate is employed in its production. Elsewhere we have also seen that the nature of a vowel can influence neighbouring sounds. With *giw*, the vowel brought the preceding consonant forward (from a velar *g* produced by contact of the tongue with the soft palate, to a hard palatal *j* produced by the tongue further forward along the roof of the mouth) en route to forming the Sanskrit verb *jīv-* (जीव्) meaning *live*. This is a standard shift in Sanskrit. We have seen the same thing in English in 1.4, where the *j* of the the infinitive suffix *–jan* palatalised the *k* of the root *tak-* to produce *teach*. It can be clearly seen in the juxtaposition of the Sanskrit adjective *ug-ra* (उग्र *strong*) and its comparative *oj-īyas* (ओजीयस् *stronger*) from *og-īyas*, where the presence of a following *ī* palatalises to *j* the *g* of the base form.

If you are agog at that, and you can be forgiven for being so, then here is the same process again with one of the most interesting verbs in English. Assuming a basic Indo-European root *gwem*, we move firstly through the First Germanic Consonant Shift to *kwem* and thence to the Gothic *qim-*, which means *come*. Indeed, it is the word *come*, which in Old English is *cum-*. Again, Latin speakers dropped the initial guttural/velar in favour of the second sound and *g-wem* went into Latin as *ven-*, as in *ven-ture*, *a-ven-ue* and *ad-ven-t*. Again the Greeks developed an initial labial and turned it into *bain-* which is the basis of *ba-sis (βά-σις)*, meaning literally a *going*. By applying the simple rules of sound change that we have established with our earlier example, we can transform the Greek *ba-sis* into its Sanskrit equivalent *ga-tis* (गतिस्). Remember that the *g* of *gwiw-os* went to *j* in *jīv-* because of the influence of the palatal vowel *ī*. In *ga-tis*, from *gwem*, the initial *g* is not followed by a palatal vowel, so it is preserved like in *ug-ra* next to *oj-īyas*.

The Sanskrit verbal root from *gwem* is *gam*, and being a class one

46

thematic verb we would expect it to form a present such as *gam-a-ti (he comes), corresponding to Old English cum-(e)-th, and Latin (g)ven-i-t. Instead we have gacch-a-ti (गच्छति). What has happened to our m, which remains in other forms of this verb such as the imperfect? Alongside the Greek root bain- there is an alternative form, ba-sk-. This sk occurs in Sanskrit as ch, and this is noted by Pāṇini in rule 7.3.77 iṣugamiyamām chaḥ (इषुगमियमां छः). This tells us that the sound ch replaces the final sound of the stems iṣ, gam and yam when a present tense ending follows, so Greek ba-sk = Sanskrit ga-ch.

The relationship of Greek sk and Sanskrit ch sheds light on another lexical network that reaches across continents and millennia. We can change the Sanskrit verbal root chid- (छिद्) into the Greek skhid- (σχιδ-). These have a basic sense of divide. The Greek present stem skhiz- (σχιζ-) leads us to schis-m (Greek σχίσ-μα). The same root appears in Gothic as skaid- and Old English as sceād-. In the latter, the initial consonants sc- are pronounced sh, which sceāw-aþ (shows) more clearly the link between Old English scip and its modern form ship. By making sc into sh, sceād becomes shed, which means separate and thence disperse in the sense that I use it in the first line of this paragraph. (The Gothic and Old English derive from the Proto-Germanic *skit- whose sense of dispersal accounts for its additional development into the word shit.) In Latin the verbal stem gains a nasal and becomes scind-, which has a past participle sciss-um which is obviously something to do with sciss-ors, instruments which cleave. But there is a red herring here which needs gutting.

In Latin, a sciss-or is not a thing that cleaves but a person who cleaves. So a pair of sciss-ors would have meant a couple of butchers. Indeed, the modern Italian verb to butcher is sgozz-are. The underlying form of our word sciss-ors is actually the same as that of chis-el. These are both traceable via modern French ciseaux to the Old French cis-oires. We now know that we are looking for a Latin verb beginning not with s but c, and what presents itself is caed-ere with its past participle caesus, meaning cut (and the source of de-cide, sui-cide and so forth). By the Middle English period, the spelling of cis-oires which was inherited from French had changed to sis-oures and this opened the way for it to be mixed up with sciss-or. A confluence of factors caused our ancestors to take the word cis-oires and respell it by analogy with a completely unrelated word – sciss-or – while retaining its original meaning. Funny people.

PART TWO

Roots

Proto-Indo-European has a basic inventory of verbal roots each of which expresses an action. These monosyllables, like the tri-consonantal roots of Semitic languages, are not themselves words. They do not occur in actual utterances. Instead, as we have seen in Part One, they are modified in various ways by accent patterns to produce a range of stems for the formation of verbs and nouns. To these stems are added prefixes and suffixes indicating number, tense, person and other information which enables us to understand how a word relates to surrounding words. A root produces a stem, and the stem in turn is made into a word. The original sounds of these roots developed differently in different languages, so to reconstruct an original Indo-European root requires that one sequence of changes be applied to, for example, its Italian descendent verb and another sequence to its English version. Meanwhile Italian's parent language Latin latterly supplied a great deal of English vocabulary, so English has its own lexicon derived from the Germanic forms of the roots as well as a Romance-based lexicon derived from the Latin forms of the same roots. The result is that, despite its extent, the larger part of English vocabulary can be traced to a group of a few dozen monosyllables by identifying which branch of Indo-European a word comes from and applying a few simple rules of sound change.

2.1

Seeing

How *idol*, *history* and *wizard* are related.

"A garden is a lovesome thing, God wot!" wrote the Manx poet Thomas Brown in his famously atrocious composition *My Garden*. That first line, the best of a mercifully small bunch, combines a pleasant if dreary initial declaration with the most delightfully dissonant squawk one would only expect to hear from a person who had temporarily lost control of their speech organs. It is possible that the writer was attacked shortly after commencing the poem, and if he wasn't then he should have been. It is at once a relief and a shame that *wot* has faded from use despite the root whence it cankerously grew awhile being otherwise rampantly productive of determinedly resilient forms. What Brown meant by *wot* was *knows* – but, "A garden is a lovesome thing, God knows!" is perfectly forgettable, even if *knows* rhymes with nice words like *rose* and *repose*. Instead Brown chose to form a chain of rhymes from *wot* to *plot* and finishing with *grot*, although having gone that far what harm could there have been in chucking in a *marmot* as well? God wot why not a marmot, but the poet used it not.

The Old English long vowel *ā* was rounded in the Middle English period to the sound represented by *oa* or *o* in words such as *loaf* and *stone* (Old English *hlāf* and *stān*). We can thus trace Brown's *wot* to the Old English *wāt* (where the vowel sounds like that in father), which serves as the first and third singular forms of the verb *wit-an* meaning *know*. The type of vowel change between the infinitive and the finite places this verb in the small but important category of preterite presents explored further in the section on auxiliary verbs in 4.3. Preterite presents use perfect forms to express essentially present tense meanings. The preterite present characteristic of this verb is not confined to Germanic languages. It is a particularly ancient feature of the same verb in Sanskrit and Greek too and this has great significance for its meaning, which we shall presently arrive at.

Before we do and before we look at some of the many imported forms, here are some examples of derivatives of *wit-an* enduring from Old English. The Old English adjective *wīs* has become *wise* and the sense of *learnedness* has been retained. Add a suffix to the adjective to get the noun *wiz-ard*, a *learned man*. In the Old Testament Book of Daniel those irritating Babylonians harass the wizard hero, who is referred to by the related word *wīt-ega* meaning *prophet*:

On Cȳres dagum cyninges wrēgdon þā Babilōniscan þone
In the days of King Cyrus the Babylonians accused the

wītegan Daniēl.
prophet Daniel.

An Old English word for *knowledge* is *witt* which we know as *wit*, and its adjective *witty* is the current form of the ancient *wittig*. Add a different suffix, the common abstract noun indicator *-ness*, to get *witness* which has an essential meaning of *knowledge* as seen in the phrase *bear witness*. Another word for *knowledge* is *wīs-dōm*, which Ælfric uses in the introduction to his *Latin Grammar*:

And ælc mann þe wīsdōm lufaþ biþ gesǣlig.
And each man who loves **wis**dom is blessed.

Returning to the origin of Brown's *wot*, the Old English *wāt* is found in the sister Germanic language of Gothic as *wáit*, seen here in the Gospel of John 15.15:

*þanaseiþs izwis ni qiþa skalkans; untē skalks ni **wáit**   ƕa*
No longer you do I call servants; for a servant knows not what

táujiþ is fráuja.
his master does.

The means by which one knows something? Seeing. This is the key to the preterite present. The reason the Old English *ic wāt* and the Gothic *ik wáit* mean *I know* is because they are past tense forms basically meaning *I saw*. Having seen something in the past allows one to know it in the present. (The meaning *see* was taken over in Germanic by the verb *see*, analysed in 1.5.) The infinitive in these languages – *wit-an* - retains the original vowel used in the original present and in words such as *wis-dom*. In Old Church Slavonic, the verb occurring in Germanic as *wit-* appears as *vid-* (*вид-*). The difference is that the Slavs kept the original vowel and the original meaning *see*, without therefore changing it into a preterite present with an extended meaning of *know*.

So, when we read in Matthew 16.28 that some shall not taste death:

dondezhe **vid**yet
until   they see (the son of man)

we are dealing with the proper present stem and the original meaning.

The Slavonic form *vid-* calls to mind the far more familiar Latin verb with the identical root – *vid-ere*, which has the first person singular present *vid-eo* meaning *I see*. As Germanic languages frequently derived words from the root *wit* by replacing the final *t* with *s*, so did Latin. The past participle *vis-us* yields a great many words in English, from *vis-ion* and *en-vis-age* to *vis-or*, *vis-a* (the neuter plural past participle meaning things that *are seen*), and the verbs *vis-it* (*go to see*) and *ad-vis-e* (corresponding to the French noun *avis* meaning *opinion* or *view*). There is a corny gag about *tele-vis-ion* being an unhappy hybrid of languages, utilising the Greek adverb *tēle* (τῆλε) meaning *afar* and the Latinate *vis-ion*. Superficially this observation is true, but the same *vid-* root appears in Greek too.

The meaning *I see* is expressed in the present by a verb quite peculiar to Greek, *hor-ō* (ὁϱῶ). The meaning *I know* is expressed by *oid-a* (οἶδα), which is marked out as a perfect tense form by the ending *a*. So, this latter is a preterite present like the *wāt* of Old English. In fact it is the *wāt* of Old English – the very same word. The past tenses of *horō* are formed on a stem *eid-* (εἰδ-) which was previously **wid-* (ϝιδ-) – the original present stem of *oida* and clearly the same root as Old English *wit-* and the Latin and Slavic *vid-*.

That the initial digamma of **wid-* is lost and the vowel lengthened to produce *eid-* must be considered fortunate given one of its derivatives. The word *id-ol* comes from the Greek *eid-ōlon* (εἴδωλον) meaning *shape* or *image – something that is seen*, and the service of idols is thus *id-olatry* (εἴδ-ωλατϱία). Had the digamma been retained and the vowel remained short (as in h*i*s, rather than f*i*ne), the Greek word would have been **widōlon* and we would call it a **widol*, which would have sounded like *widdle*. And J.Milton Hayes might never have written his poem that begins, "There's a little yellow idol to the north of Kathmandu". From the Greek sense of seeing comes *id-ea* (ἰδ-έα), a *look* or *semblance* of a thing. Derived from the sense of knowing is *history* (ἱσ-τοϱία) from **hid-tor-* (**ἰδ-τοϱ-). In Sanskrit too the verb *vid-* (विद्) is a preterite present, and as with the Greek the form usually used

with a present meaning of *know* – *veda* (वेद), corresponding to Greek *oid-a* - is marked out as a perfect form by ending in *a*. The foundational

51

literature of India is the collection of sacred books in Sanskrit known as the *Ved-as*.

There is another productive root with a sense of vision. The Latin word for *bird* is *avis*, as in *avian*, and the verb *look* is *spec-ere*. The compound of *avis* and *spec-* gives English the word *au-spic-ious*, an adjective to describe something that points to a bright future. It was first used to describe the activities of the Roman seers who read bird intestines like tea leaves. Of course not all seers saw such signs as we should say seemed auspicious, as Julius Caesar found out on the Ides of March. The Greek form of the same verb switches the consonants, turning *spec-* into *skep-* (whence *scep-tic*, meaning *one who considers*) and spawning the word *scope*, which is often compounded. For example, *micro-scope*, *peri-scope*, and *bi-shop*. The latter (Old English *bi-scop*) is a trimmed form of the Greek *epi-scop-os* (ἐπί-σκοπ-ος) meaning *overseer*.

2.2

Being

**How *be*, *is*, and *was* come from three different verbs.
And if *was*, why *were*?**

One of the most obviously common features of many Indo-European languages is the verb expressed in English as *be*. For example, the third person plural present *they are*:

French – *sont*
German – *sind*
Latin – *sunt*
Sanskrit – *santi* (सन्तिं)
Old English – *sindon*
Greek – *eisin* (εἰσίν)

When there is such inter-lingual similarity, how did modern English come to have a verb whose infinitive and past participles are *be* and *been*, whose present tense consists of *am, is* and *are*, and whose past tense is *was* and *were*? It is a discombobulous thing, but the discombobulousness is not confined to English. The concept of existence has been discombobbling along for thousands of years, and we must not be surprised for it is a complex one which has exercised the minds of many great and boring people. It is beyond the scope of the current work to recombobulate the how or why or when we ceased to be lexically combobulant regarding existence, as we are here rather concerned with the what. So, what?

French, from Latin, inherited the two *essent*ial ancient verbs meaning *be*. The one that produced the third person plural forms listed above is Latin *es-se* (French *ê-tre* whose circumflex points to an earlier form **es-tre*) which appears in Sanskrit as *as* (अस्). The ancestor of these forms is what gives English the present tense *am*: Sanskrit *asmi* (अस्मि), Latin *sum* from **es[u]mi*. Also *is*: French, Latin *est*, German *ist*, Sanskrit *asti* (अस्ति), Greek *esti* (ἐστί). It also supplies the English plural *are*, which is actually the same word as all the *sunts* and *santis* in our first list. How so?

The Greek name for the later *r* is *rho* (ϱ). The process by which the sounds *s* or *z* become *r* is rhotacism, and it is this that is responsible for the clouding of the waters here. At an early stage in the development of some languages, an *s* or *z* that occurred between vowels became an *r* if the accent did not immediately precede it. This rhotacism is one of a series of changes identified in the late nineteenth century by the Danish linguist Karl Verner and linked to the Second Germanic Consonant Shift. Each change in this series is due to the accent occurring after a particular sound, when that sound occurs between vowels (see 1.5 for the treatment of intervocalic *h* in the verb *see*). You notice it in modern English in pairs such as *éxecute/exécutor*, and *ábsolute/absólve*, where the *x* and *s* are voiced when the stress does not immediately precede them.

In Latin, for example, the third person present of *esse* is *és-t*, but the future form is *er-ít*. In the future form the accent is shifted from the *é* before the *s* to the *í* after it, and this triggers rhotacism which changes the now intervocalic *s* to *r*, giving *er-it*. (See 2.4 for another example of this in the verbs *rise* and *rear*.) Similarly, English *are* is based on something like **esén-ti*, where the *-ti* has dropped off to leave **esén*, and as with the Latin the accent falls after the *s* so it becomes the *r* in **erén*. Because the first vowel is unaccented the sound is fairly indistinct and it is easy to see how an unstressed *e* (which at this stage of the language would have been pronounced like the vowel in *set*) might come to be conflated in pronunciation and spelling with *a* and leave us with **arén*. The later tendency for word stress in Germanic languages to shift to the first syllable led to the weakening of nearly all inflectional endings and all trace of the final *n* disappeared. The result of all these stages since our presumed most ancient trisyllabic **esénti* is the minimalist monosyllable *are*.

If that is the history of the word *are*, then where does *sindo-n*, which appears in our first list as an Old English form, fit in? This is down to dialect. I cited *sindo-n* to show an obvious connection between several languages. But *sindon* occurred chiefly in the West Saxon dialect and ultimately lost out to the Mercian *earun* which is the attested form of our reconstructed **erén* above. Both *sindon* and *earun* come from our prototype **esénti*, and they have both developed because of the accent being on the second syllable. With *sindo-n* the unaccented first syllable dropped off and it developed from the *-sent* of **e-sént-i* (in a process that roughly went **e-sénti-* > **sénti-* > *sindon*). With *earun* the unaccented first syllable caused rhotacism and it developed from the *esen-*

54

of *esén-ti (*esén-ti- > *erén-ti- > earun). This verb is used to denote existence – 'There *is* a house in New Orleans...'

I said that French inherited two essential verbs from Latin. One was *esse*, as we have seen, which Latin used for forms based on the present stem, namely the present, imperfect and future. The other was *fuisse*, which Latin used for its perfect forms and French uses in the past simple and imperfect subjunctive. But English has this verb too. *fu-* is historically the same word as *be*, and they both derive from a root *bheu*.

The initial *bh-* sound, which is preserved in Sanskrit *bhu* (भु), is an aspirated form of the English *b*. In Latin and Greek the sound *bh* lost its voicing but retained its aspiration, softening to *f* in Latin and *ph* (φ) in Greek (see 2.9 for more examples). In Germanic languages, however, it retained its voicing but lost its aspiration, hardening to *b*. In Greek, this verbal root *phu-* (φυ-) is the basis for English forms like *phy-sical*. From the Latin we get *fu-ture*. In English, we have the forms *be*, *being*, *been*.

What's the difference? Why were there two verbs in the first place? There was originally a clear difference in meaning and use between the two. The standard theory is that while the ancestor of *is* meant what it does today, the ancestor of *be* had more of a sense of *become*. (However, it had nothing to do with the *be-* in *become*, which is another tale). This theory seems to hold water if we examine usage in Sanskrit, but the search continues for further clarification.

Although we have put the Romance languages to bed, we still have to explain *was* and *were*, which come from yet another verb that we can trace back to Sanskrit. This time, the root is *vas* (वस्) which means *dwell* and is mostly used to express where someone or something lives. This verb popped up in Old English as the stem used to form a past tense of the *as* and *be* verbs. You will notice again the alternation of *s* and *r* in the forms *was* and *wer-e* – rhotacism due to accent. *vas* found its way into Greek to generate several comfortable words like *hes-tia* (ἑστία) meaning *hearth*. Talking of hearths, the Roman goddess of the hearth is *Ves-ta* of the famous virgins, and a slave born at their master's house was a *ver-na* (from *ves-i-na*), and they probably spoke in the *vernacular* i.e. the dialect of the place where they dwelt.

55

2.3

Sitting

In provocative ways

Throughout this book are references to the Indian grammarian Pāṇini and his opus on Sanskrit grammar. The brevity of the sutras and the consequent need for extensive interpretation justifies the view of the visionary eighteenth century orientalist Sir William Jones, said to have described the work as, "dark as the darkest oracle." Learning or understanding it without a guru is practically impossible. Thus the tradition of studying Sanskrit grammar in India is most ancient and of cosmic importance, for a word of the sacred language mispronounced or misformed by a chanting brahmin during a ritual blocks the efficacy of that ritual and it must be performed again. One of the most famous exponents of Pāṇinian grammar was the seventh century teacher Bhaṭṭi. He would spend his days filling the mortal vessels that were his students with the eternal knowledge of the great Pāṇini. One day an elephant ambled into class, and as this pachyderm's perambulations disrupted the delivery of knowledge, lessons had to be suspended for a year according to custom. So that his students would not suffer too much from the hiatus, Bhaṭṭi composed an abbreviated version of the Indian epic *Rāmāyaṇa* and inserted into its verses examples of Pāṇinian rules. Known as the *Bhaṭṭikāvyam* (*Bhaṭṭi's poem*) this has rarely been translated out of Sanskrit because the purpose of the text – to illuminate points of Sanskrit grammar – is lost in another language.

There are, however, a couple of obtainable English translations. They grapple gamely with the slippery task of rendering the highly ornate Sanskrit sentences intelligible, but in one of them the reader is distracted – charmed, amused, admiring of the translator's efforts, but distracted nevertheless – by sentences such as, "She tried to squat in an indecent way." To cut a long story short as Bhaṭṭi did, in the *Rāmāyaṇa* the hero Rāma is propositioned by a female demon called Śūrpaṇakhā, and in a misguided effort to seduce him she "tries to squat in an indecent way." Rāma is having none of it and cuts off her nose and ears. The episode is related by Bhaṭṭi thus:

तस्याः   सासद्यमानाया   लोलूयावानरघूततमः
tasyāḥ sāsadyamānāyā lolūyāvānraghūttamaḥ

असिं   कौक्षेयमुद्यम्य   चकारापनसं   मुखम्
asiṃ kaukṣeyamudyamya cakārāpanasaṃ mukham.

I shall proceed to mutilate this one verse which means: "Resolved to chop, the best of the Raghus (Rāma) raised his sword and made nose-less the face of she who was crouching (lewdly)", or in strict word order; "Of she who was crouching (lewdly) desiring to chop the Raghu-highest (his) sword having raised made noseless the face." This is not the end of his problems but we shall leave him there and note the word *sāsadyamānāyā*, which is the feminine genitive singular present participle of the reduplicated intensive form of the verb *sad* (सद्), and can be translated, "of she who was crouching lewdly."

There's a bit of indecent squatting going on in the Book of Revelation too, and below we see the same verb in its Latin form *sed*. In 17.3-5, the seer is carried into the wilderness:

*et   vidi mulierem **sed**entem super bestiam coccineam,*
And I saw a woman **sit**ting   on a   scarlet beast (which was)

Plenam nominibus blasphemiae, habentem capita septem et
full of the names of blasphemy, having seven heads and

cornua decem....et in fronte eius   nomen scriptum:
and ten horns....And on her forehead a name was written:

Mysterium: Babylon magna,   mater fornicationem, et
Mystery,   Babylon the Great, Mother of Harlots and

abominationem terrae.
of the Abominations of the Earth.

At this point the abuse of the Babylonians, as relentless as it is humourless, perhaps reaches a zenith of hysteria. Throughout the Bible they have lashed upon them some of the most dramatic curses. Isaiah 14 rips into an unnamed Babylonian tyrant who, by a twist of translation and interpretation through several languages and centuries, comes to be identified with no less than the Devil himself. This passage, suffused with heartstopping imagery of damnation, has provided inspiration for works as diverse as William Langland's Middle English allegorical masterpiece *Piers the Plowman*, where it is worked into chapter two of the dream narrative, and the 1976 reggae song *I Chase the Devil* by Max Romeo and Lee 'Scratch' Perry, later sampled by the dance group Prodigy. The song opens, as does the gobbet below, with the second line of Isaiah 14.12, quoting the New King James Bible, which rather flexibly interprets the Latin to spectacular effect:

O Lucifer, son of the morning!
How you are cut down to the ground,
You who weakened the nations!
For you have said in your heart:
'I will ascend into heaven,
I will exalt my throne above the stars of God:
I will also **sit** on the mount of the congregation
On the farthest sides of the north.

Translated into Latin, we find that the penultimate line contains a recognisable form of the same verb:

sed-ebo in monte testamenti

The Sanskrit *sad* and the Latin *sed* are cognate with the English *sit* and the Russian *sid- (сид)*. The Latin vowel takes us to the Greek which turns the initial sound into an aspirate to make a root *hed- (ἑδ-)* and a verbal stem *hez(d)- (ἑζ-)*. A Greek noun meaning *seat* is *hedos*. The prefix *kata (κατα)*, meaning *down* and occurring in *cata-stophe (κατα-στροφή)* – literally a *turning* or *throwing down* - when placed before an aspirate becomes *kath- (καθ-)*. With a slight tweak we can compound it with our word for *seat* to make *kath-ed-ra (καθ-ἑδ-ρα)*. A *cathedral* is a place where a bishop has his throne, on which he sits down. In a typical process of simplification the medial consonants of *cathedral* were eroded over time to become Middle English *chaiere* and the modern word *chair*. The Latin form is highly productive, yielding words from the obvious – *sed-ent-ary*, inclined to *sit*; *pre-sid-ent*, one *sitting* foremost – to the slightly less so – *session*, a *sitting* (from the past participle *sess-us*), and *in-sid-ious*, *sitting* in wait to commit some treachery. Rather like squatting indecently.

58

Standing

The small difference between *president* and *prostitute*. And why do we *rear* children?

The Old Testament tells us that God created the waters on the third day (see 2.11). There then arose the question of what to call it. Not a pressing question as God had not yet created anyone who might need to refer to it, but name it he regardless did. Sadly that name is lost to us. When he later eyeballed the builders of Babel getting busy on the Great Ziggurat of Babylon, he permanently banjaxed linguistic unity and at a stroke created an entirely new business sector called translation. Consequently the christening of the waters of Genesis 1.10 is related thus in Latin, Greek and Sanskrit where the words in italic and bold correspond to the same in the English translation, "…(and) the collection *of waters* he called **seas**":

…congregationesque *aquarum* appellavit **maria**

…καὶ τὰ συστήματα τῶν *ὑδάτων* ἐκάλεσεν **θαλάσσας**
…kai to sustēmata tōn *hudatōn* ekalesen **thalassas**

… *तोय*राशेर्नाम **समुद्र** इति कृतवान्
…*toya*rāśernāma **samudra** iti kṛtavān

The confounding of languages was, rather like the Ziggurat itself, incomplete. In 3.1 it is shown that the *ud-* of Sanskrit *sam-udra* and the *hud-* of Greek *hud-atōn* are the same as the *wat-* of English *wat-er* and that the *aq-* of Latin *aq-ua* is related to the *is-* of *is-land*. However, that the words used for the name of the waters viz. *mare* (*maria* is plural), *thalassa* (or *thalatta* in Attic Greek) and *samudra* (literally *together-water* and one of the commoner of the myriad terms for ocean in Sanskrit) are completely unrelated to one another shows that there was nevertheless significant fallout from Babel. And it also points to the possible geographical origin of the people who spoke the prehistoric ancestral languages that became the Indo-European group (assuming for a moment that the story is a bit more complicated than the Old Testament suggests).

The oldest stratum of vocabulary shared by Indo-European languages may be an indication of who these people were, where they were from and what they did. For example, in 3.3 we see that the words for *cow* and *ox* in several Indo-European languages are basically the same, or at least clearly derived from common roots. This suggests that the speakers of the ancestral languages were probably farmers or herders for whom cattle were a fundamental part of life. Conversely, had they been fishermen we might expect to find a common word for *sea* because that would have been fundamental. We do not. Instead, radiating from an inland region – as yet undetermined and the subject of lengthy debate, although plausibly somewhere in what is now southern Russia – the ancestors of the Indians found the Indian Ocean or the Arabian Sea and gave it a name, the ancestors of the Greeks found the Mediterranean and gave it a different name, the ancestors of the Italians found the same sea and gave it yet another name, while the ancestors of the Teutons found another one and called it the *sea*.

In the quotations above, the words I have translated as *collection* are the Latin *congregatio*, the Sanskrit *rāśi* and the Greek *sustēma*. Although these are also completely different words, the Greek contains a root which is found throughout Indo-European. The Greek word finds its way into English as *system*. It is a compound of the prefix *sun-* (meaning *together*, see 2.11) and a derivation from the verb *i-stē-mi* (*ῐ́-στη-μι*), meaning to *cause to stand*. The full form *sun-istē-mi* occurs as a verb meaning *put together* or *combine*. The *stē* of *i-stē-mi* is related to the *sta* in *sta-nd* and this element forms part of hundreds of words in modern English. As it appears in *i-stē-mi* so it does in other Greek-derived words such as *ec-sta-sy* (*ἔκ-στα-σις* – literally a *standing apart*) and the name *Ana-sta-sia* (from *ἀνά-στα-σιο* – *awakening* or, in the Bible, *resurrection*).

The direct Latin equivalent of *sun-istē-* is *con-si-ste-*. Like the Greek this takes the combinative prefix *con-* (*sun-*) and a stem derived from the *sta-nd* verb with a causative sense, in this case *si-st-ere*. The derivative stem is formed according to a common Indo-European pattern in which the verbal root syllable – in this Latin example *stā* – is duplicated to the left (reduplicated) i.e. the duplicated syllable occurs before the root, not after. From *stā-re* (a first conjugation verb identified by the *ā* in that infinitive) to *siste-re* (a third conjugation verb identified by the short *e* in its infinitive), we thus begin with an initial stage of **stā-stā-*. The highly regular rules governing the form of reduplicated syllables in most languages do not, however, allow for them to feature a consonant cluster. Hence the *t* of the reduplicated syllable is dropped leaving **sā-*

stā-. Further rules determine the alternation of vowels and these weaken *ā* to *i* giving **si-stā*. But our derivative is not **sistā-re* but *siste-re*; the second person singular present indicative of the simple verb is *stā-s* (you stand), but the same part of the derivative is not **sistā-s* but *sisti-s*. The prefixing of the reduplicated syllable has weakened the second syllable and the verb has ceased to look like a first conjugation verb and drifted into the third. (The same phenomenon accounts for the different vowels in the words *fac-t* and *per-fec-t* – the prefix *per* adds a syllable and the following vowel is weakened as a result. We can also compare *fac-ile* and *dif-fic-ult* < **dis-fac-ult*) So the stem of *con-si-st*, *in-si-st*, *as-si-st* and so on developed by:

stā- > *stā-stā- > *sā-stā- > *si-stā > si-st

The same rules of reduplication also explain the Greek. As in the Latin there is a long root vowel in *stē* which is weakened in the reduplicated syllable to *i* giving *i-stē*. A distinctive feature of the Greek form is that it is not **si-stē* but *i-stē* – it has lost the initial consonant of the reduplicated syllable. In Latin, we have seen that there is a simple verb *sta-re* and a derivative *si-ste-re*. In Greek, the reduplicated form does service for both simple and causative meanings. *i-stē-mi* has a basic meaning of *I sta-nd* when used intransitively, and *I cause to sta-nd* when used transitively. The unreduplicated form of the verb, with its original *a* vowel, does not occur as widely in Greek (although the future stem drops the reduplicated syllable) but there are some important nouns which derive from it. We have seen *ec-sta-sy* and *Ana-sta-sia*. There is also *sta-dium,* a Latinised form of the Greek *sta-dion* (στά-διον).

Sanskrit deals with this verb in a slightly different way again. The root is *sthā* (सुथा) but the present stem is the reduplicated *ti-ṣṭha-* (तष्ठि). Like the Latin, there is a change of vowel in the reduplicated syllable. However, unlike the Latin *si-st-* which uses the first consonant of the root – *s* – in the reduplicated syllable, Sanskrit uses the second – *th*. It normally follows the same pattern as Latin, but where there is a non-nasal consonant - here *th* - preceded by a sibilant – *s* – it takes the second consonant of the root – in this case *th* – giving initially **thi-sth-*. Further sound rules then come into play. In **thi-sth-* (in which *th* is not a fricative like the *th* in ma*th*s but an aspirated stop like the *th* in goat-*h*erd) there are aspirated consonants in consecutive syllables – **thi-sth-*. This cannot occur, so the first one loses its aspiration resulting in **ti-sth-*. The same rule applies in Greek, and is known as Grassmann's

Law after the nineteenth century German philologist Hermann Grassmann. A further rule states that after certain vowels, including *i*, certain
consonants are changed from dental to retroflex, which is to say that
they are produced further back in the mouth. The *s* of *ti-sth-* thus becomes *ṣ* (curl your tongue up and say *sh*), and the *th* becomes *ṭh* (the
very distinctive South Asian soft consonant sound). The result, with a
shortened root vowel, is *ti-ṣṭha-* by:

sthā   >   *thi-stha-   >   *ti-stha-   >   ti-ṣṭha-

Reduplication was used widely in the formation of perfect stems. It
is an almost untraceably distant feature of some English verbs. It is only
really understood in English through juxtaposition with Gothic. The
preterite of the Old English verb *hātan* (to call) is usually *hēt* (he
called). There are some instances, however, of *he-ht*. The repetition of *h*
marks this as a contracted version of a form seen fully in Gothic as *hai-
háit*. By the time of the earliest recorded English the reduplicated stems
had mostly collapsed back into monosyllables. The few surviving verbs
which originally belonged to this group include *let* and *hang*, but they
have all undergone further complex and substantial changes which have
totally obscured the relationship to their ancient reduplicated forms.

English also has a sprinkling of causative derivatives. They do not
reduplicate like *i-stē-mi* but rather employ a common derivational affix.
This occurs in Germanic languages as *j/ij*, which we have seen elsewhere (see 1.3) is pronounced *y* and used in plural suffixation to create
alternations such as *mouse* and *mice*. To make a causative, this affix
was added to the form of the verb containing the ablaut adjusted vowel
characteristic of the preterite. For example, the verb *rīs-an* (to *rise*) has
a preterite form *rās* (*ros-e*) featuring the same pattern of vowel change
as *wit-an* and *wāt* in 2.1. The addition of the *j* affix then causes i-
mutation of the back vowel *ā* to make *ræs-*. In 2.2 we saw how the
rhotacism of the Second Germanic Consonant Shift *s* to *r* where the
accent did not fall on the syllable immediately preceding *s*, which accounts for pairs such as *was/were* and *is/are*. The causative suffix always took the accent, which turned the *s* of *ræs-* into r and produced
the verb *rær-an*. This survives in Modern English as rear, which has a
restricted use in idioms such as *rear its ugly head* and *child-rearing*
where it means *cause to rise*. So the process is:

*rās-ján   >   *ræs-ján   >   *rær-ján   >   rær-an   >   rear

However, the far more common causative of *rise* is *raise*, which clearly has not undergone rhotacism. But it is not actually an English word. It is a later import from Scandinavian languages which had not experienced the Second Germanic Consonant Shift. It is nevertheless a regularly derived causative from an original intransitive verb and matches the Gothic causative *ráis-jan* based on a presumed **reis-an*.

In Gothic there is a causative of our *stand* verb, *ana-stod-jan* (with the same *ana* prefix as Greek *ana-sta-sis*, cognate with English *on*) which again is based on the preterite form (equivalent to English *stood*). The same derivational affix responsible for these English and Gothic derivatives is used to form causatives in Sanskrit, and it requires the same conditions. The causative affix *–aya-* (the Germanic *–j-*) is added to (usually) an ablaut adjusted stem. Our root *sthā* - whose reduplicated present form is *ti-ṣṭha-ti* (तिष्ठति *he stands*) - adds a *p* before the causative suffix to become *sthā-p-aya-ti* (स्थापयति *I cause to stand*).

That reduplication was a major feature of our *stand* verbs is clear from the above examples in Latin, Greek and Sanskrit. In contrast, the English verb *sta-nd* does not appear to have been subject to reduplication. It does have its foibles, though. It is unusual to find the letter *n* in the present tense of the finite verb. It is there in English and Icelandic but not in German or the Scandinavian languages. The *n* was there in the past participle of Old English – *sta-nden* – but that form was suppleted by the preterite *stood* (Old English *stōd*). Nor do the Old English nouns derived from this verb use the *n*. The word *stō-w* meaning *place* features in place names like *Godstow* and *Stow on the Wold*. The Old English *ste-de* survives in *Hamp-stead* and *Berkham-sted*, but is far more prevalent in mainland Europe where, for example, the German form *Sta-dt* means *town* or *city*.

However, most of the English words from this root came to us through other languages after the Anglo-Saxon period. In 2.3 we saw that the Latin verb *sed-* (*sit*) combines with the prefix *pre-* to form *pre-sid-ent* (the change of vowel due to the rule of weakening triggered by the addition of a syllable, explained above with reference to *stā-s* and *si-st-is*). The perfect stem of *stā-re* (*stand*) is *stet-*. When this is preceded by the prefix *pro-* it becomes *stit-*. Given that the prefixes *pro* and *pre* are the same and have a sense of *for-ward* or *pro-minence*, the only difference between a *pre-sid-ent* and a *pro-stit-ute* seems to be that the former is sitting and the latter standing. The Latin root is almost swallowed up by other elements in words like *contra-st* (a standing against), and a pair of official terms – *ar-re-st* (from *ad-re-stā-re*, essentially meaning *remain*) and *con-sta-ble* (a contraction of *comes sta-bulī*, meaning Count of the Stables).

63

2.5

Moving

Whelks **and** *vulvas.*

The great chronicler of the Anglo-Saxon period the Venerable Bede's literary output includes the *Ecclesiastical History* and the *Lives of the Abbots of Wearmouth and Jarrow*. His protégé Egbert went on to become Archbishop of York and helped that northern city become a centre of English scholarship. Bede is a central and dynamic figure in the history and historiography of Britain, and no child should enter secondary education without this excellent man's exciting and elevated existence their exemplar, his wisdom and intellectual rigour their companion, and his unceasing curiosity their inspiration. For through Bede we can know our country and feel its ancient history as closely as a fetid Anglo-Saxon breath on our faces. And through Bede we can know our Atlantic dogwinkles. Even as Yemen was the myrrh-producing capital of the ancient world and still produces tons of the stuff today, so Britain could now be known the world over for its dogwinkles had we doggedly winkled away at that traditional cottage industry. We did not, and must therefore turn to the great chronicler for enlightenment.

Dogwinkle is, of course, a later term. Were it not I still doubt that Bede in his Venerability would have used it. He called them whelks. Everyone remembers their first whelk and I am sure I shall too. In the meantime it suffices to read about them, particularly in Bede's Old English with its thick, moist vocabulary. Describing Britain in his *Ecclesiastical History*, he says:

hēr bēoþ oft numene   missenlicra cynna **weoloc**- *sciella   and*
here are often caught diverse kinds of **whelk**-shells and

musculan, and on þǣm   bēoþ oft gemētte thā betstan
mussels, and from them are often obtained the best

meregrotan ǣlces hīwes. And her bēoþ swīthe
pearls   of all hues. And here are   very

genyhtsume **weolacas**, *of þǣm bith gewohrt se* **weoloc**-*rēada telg, thone*

64

abundant **whelks**, from which is worked that **whelk**-red   dye, that

ne maeg ne sunne blǣcan,   ne ne regen wierdan;
neither may the sun bleach, nor the rain damage;

ac swā hē bith ealdra, swā hē faegerra bith.
and as it   is older   so it is fairer (i.e. more beautiful).

So, what's a whelk? Note the different spelling in the Old and Modern English words. The first thing you notice is that an *h* has crept in. This seems to be due to analogy with an unrelated and archaic word *whelk* which is a term for a small pimple. We have, then, *weoloc*, as a term for a mollusc with a spiral shell. Another term for a spiral is *helix*, which is actually the same word as *weoloc*. *Helix* (ἕλιξ) is an Ancient Greek word - meaning *spiral* - but the initial *h* is not the original sound. That, in even more ancient Greek, was a *w*, represented in writing as a digamma (roughly *F*). So, instead of *helix* we have *welix*. And, as *x* actually represents *k + s* it would be more accurate to say that *welix* is actually *welik-s* - which is very whelky, or weolocy. Having reconstructed the Greek to accord with the Old English, we can now see how the Greek verbal root *hel-*, which would originally have begun with a digamma and been *wel-,* is related to the Latin root *vol(v)-* (pronounced *wol(w)*) meaning *turn* or *roll*. The Latin provides many modern words such as *vulv-a*, *re-volve* and *re-volu-tion, e-volve*, and *volu-me* (something written on a roll of paper).

It is fitting that *whelk*, being the name of a sea creature, is related to many other water-associated words. From the verb's sense of a turning motion it comes to be applied naturally to water. Hence water is drawn from a *well* (Old English *wella*). When water moves it creates ripples, or ridges, and the shape of these inspired the *wale* in *gunwale*, meaning the ridge or plank on the side of a ship where, originally, guns were situated. In King Lear, Edgar conjures up a fiend whose eyes:

were two full moons; he had a thousand noses,
horns *whelkt* and waved like the enridged sea.

It is not fitting, though it is quite true, that *whelk*, being the name of a creature that has no legs, is also related to the English verb *walk*. Compare the Old English form of the mollusc's appellation, *weoloc*, with *wēolc*, which is the past participle of the Old English verb *wealc-an*, meaning *walk*. Old English has broken the root vowel before *l* (see 1.4 and 1.5), while Gothic preserves the simple vowel *a*, as in this extract from the Gospel of Mark, rendered into Gothic by the 4th century bishop Wulfila:

Jah warth skūra windis mikila jah wēgōs **waltitēdun** *in skip,*
And there arose a great storm and waves **rolled** against the ship,

swaswē ita juthan gafullnōda.
so   it already became full.

    Another root with the same initial sound and a meaning of movement displays a similar pattern of development in these languages. The word *way* is the modern form of Old English *weg* which comes from a root meaning *carry* and is related to *weigh-t*. The *h* of *weigh-t* hints at the original stem-final. Its Latin counterpart is *veh-* > *veh-icle*, whose past participle stem produces *vec-tor*. The Latin is almost identical to the widely used Sanskrit root *vah-*. The Greek, as with *whelk* and *helix*, drops the initial *w* from **woxh-os* (Fóχ-oς) to produce *oxh-os* (ὄχ-oς) meaning *chariot*.

    This pattern of English *w*, Latin and Sanskrit *v*, and Greek elision is also seen in the root behind an element in many English place names. The name *Wick* occurs in several parts of England and it also forms part of many other place names, such as *Wig-an* and *Gat-wick*. In English names it generally denotes a place where there is a farm, so *Gat-wick* basically means *goat farm*. The Old English noun *wīc* has a broad sense of *place* or *dwelling* and probably comes into the language from Latin *vic-us* meaning *village*, which also produces *vic-inus* (*neighbour*) > *vic-inity* (and French *vois-in*). This is a very common verbal root in Sanskrit where it appears as *viś-* (वश्) meaning *enter*, and the Latin *neighbour* noun *vīc-us* is *veś-aḥ* (वेश:). Once again Greek deletes the initial *w* so **woik-os* (Foîx-oς) > *oik-os* (oîx-oς) meaning *house*.

2.6

Making

Kings and *genitals*

Royalty and commoners - is there any substantial difference? If the substance is money, yes. On a molecular level, I don't believe so. Philologically no. The origins of the word *king* become clearer when we place it alongside its modern German equivalent *König*. This retains the disyllabic structure of its ancestor which occurs in Old English as *cyning*. There are two elements here, *cyn-* and *-ing*. The first one first.

The Old English word *cynn* (where the initial *c* is pronounced as a hard *k*), meaning *tribe* or *race*, has been respelt in Modern English as *kin*, which these days has a restricted idiomatic application in phrases like *next of kin*. Its broader application in Old English – reflected in the alternative and far commoner modern form *kin-d* - is seen in *Beowulf*, when the heroes behold the fearsome lake that is home to the monstrous Grendel:

*gesāwon ðā æfter wætere   wyrm-***cynnes** *fela*
they saw   through the water many   **kinds** of serpents

In Gothic, which illuminates so much of Old English, the word corresponding to *cynn* was *kuni*, where the final *i* becomes *j* (pronounced *y*) in all forms except the nominative singular due to i-umlaut (see 1.3). So, if we want to say *of the tribe* using the genitive singular ending *-is*, we move from *kuni* through an intermediate stage *kuni-is* en route to the actual form *kunj-is*. This *i/j* disappears as we move westward from Gothic to Old English, but its former presence is indicated by the effect it had on the preceding vowel, turning the *u* of *kuni* into the *y* of *cynn* (compare *mūs* and *mȳs* in 1.3). It also caused the lengthening of the consonant *n*, which is consequently represented as *nn* in *cynn*. Why this digression into Gothic?

It shows an important stage in connecting the English *king* from *cyning* to what lies even further east than Gothic. In 1.2 we saw how the First Germanic Consonant Shift changed an original Proto-Indo-European *k* to *h*, thus accounting for Greek *kard-* and English *heart*. It also changed an original *g* to *k* (also see 1.6). This correspondence is seen in an unrelated word that looks very similar to our root - English *kn-ee* answers to Latin *gen-u* (as in *genu-flect*) and Greek *gon-u* (γόν-υ as in *hexa-gon*). So the Gothic *kun-* derives theoretically from **gun*. The *u* in Gothic *kun* is a weakened form of an original *e*. If we apply these two changes to *kun* it becomes *gen*. And from here we can begin to see the immense *gen-erative* power of Indo-European roots.

Beginning as far away from England as we can, the root *gen*, which has an essential meaning of *produce* or *beget* occurs in Sanskrit as *jan* (जन्). While original *g* changed to *k* in English, it changed to *j* further east, so the Sanskrit equivalent of English *kn-ee*, Latin *gen-u* and Greek *gon-u* is *jan-u* (जनु). In typically poetic manner, Sanskrit employs this root in such words as *aṇḍa-ja* (अण्डज), which literally translates as *eggborn* and is a particularly delightful way of referring to a bird. Here it is used in the love story of King Nala and Damayanti, part of the great Sanskrit epic the *Mahābhārata*. Nala employs a goose (see 1.1 for more on the Sanskrit word for *goose*) as a messenger to Damayanti. The goose-messenger is a famous motif in classical Indian love stories, and here the epic eggy envoy has just received Damayanti's response to Nala's proposition:

तथेत्युक्त्वाण्डजः   कन्यां   वदिर्भसुय   वशिाम्पते
tathetyuktvāṇḍajaḥ   kanyāṃ vidarbhasya viśāmpate
"so be it", said the eggborn to the daughter of Vidarbha's king

One of the many terms for a lotus flower is *paṅka-ja* (पङ्कज), meaning *mudborn*.

Between Greek and Latin and their descendants, which share the *gen* form (Greek *gen-os*, Latin *gen-us* meaning *type*), we find many words of type and becoming. *Gen-re* is the same as *gen-der* - the *d* in the latter word being a peculiarly English addition. The Latin *gen* meaning *people*, which is fully *gen(t)s*, brings forth directly and through French the words *gen-tle*, *gen-teel* and *gen-tile*, which are all basically the same. The connection to *gen-s* in meaning is that people of one's own *kin* or *gen-us* are noble and honourable, and this mirrors the use of the English equivalent *kin-d* to mean both *type* and *friendly*. Hence also *gen-try* and *gen-erous* amongst others. Returning to the fundamental meaning of the root, we also get words connoting *gen-eration*, such as *gen-ital*.

68

So, our public figurehead the *king* we find to be related to certain private parts. But we began by saying that the Old English word consisted of two elements, *cyn* and *ing*. We have accounted for the first, so what of the second? It is a suffix denoting *belonging to*. A *king*, then, belongs to the *kin*. He is a son of the tribe, and indeed one of us.

2.7

Baking

Linking *dough*, *fiction* and *paradise*. The relationship between *female* and *fellate*, *vagina* and *vanilla*.

Bread – not to be confused with *bred*. *Bred* is the past participle of *breed*. A noun derived from *breed* is *brood*, which looks a bit like the German word *Brot*, which means *bread*. So let the fog of confusion not hang here.

Bread is a noble thing. Whereas a poor man might only stretch to a slice, a rich man would likely lust for a loaf. Naturally so, given that the word *lord* is a contraction of the Old English *hlāf-ord*, itself a contraction of the compound **hlāf-weard*. The first element of this compound is *hlāf*, the ancestor of our word *loaf* and the German *Laib*. There is a pattern of substitution of *f* and *b* accounting for differing final consonants in *loaf* and *Laib* (which also accounts for English *have* against the German *habe*) and both have lost the initial aspirate *h* (see 1.2 for more on the loss of initial *h* in consonant clusters). In modern Russian, that initial aspirate remains as *xh*, producing *xhleb (хлеб)*, as seen in *Matthew* 4.4 here in Old Church Slavonic:

*ne   o   **xlěbě** edinomĭ poživetŭ člověkŭ*
not by a **loaf**   alone   lives   man

The second element of *hlāf-ord*, the *–ord*, is a truncated form of *weard*. This occurs in modern English as *ward* and *warden* (along with the cognate French-derived *guard* and *guard-ian*). This is a common word in Old English, and in the example below the epic hero *Beowulf* uses it to address King Hrothgar in rousing him to avenge the murder of his counsellor Æschere (where *rīce* answers to the modern German *Reich*):

*Ārīs,   rīces   **weard***
Arise, kingdom's **guard**ian

A lord is someone who looks after the baps, a keeper of the crumpet, a muffin master, providing security to scones and protection to pancakes. Further, the name Edward means guardian of the wealth – *Ed-*

from Anglo-Saxon *ead* meaning prosperity. So, if the English actor Edward Woodward had been made a Lord, his name with title would mean Breadkeeper Wealthkeeper Woodkeeper. Had he lived fifteen hundred years ago he would have been called *Hlāf-weard Ead-weard Wudu-weard*. Now there's a stage name for the brave.

If the *hlāf-ord* looks after the bread, who makes it? The *hlāf-dige* – which similarly contracts into modern English as *lady*. The essential meaning of the word *lady* is *breadmaker*. We know the *hlāf-* of *hlāfdige* is *loaf*, so what can be conjured up from *–dige*? This verb occurs in Gothic as *dig-an*, meaning *knead*, and the related Old English noun *dāh* gives us the modern English *dough*. (Bread and women are associated in a different way in Urdu, where forms of the word *chapati* (چپاتی), widely used to refer to a well kneaded flat bread, is also a term for a lesbian or lesbian activity.) The Gothic root *dig-* is virtually identical to its Sanskrit equivalent *dih-* (दिह्) meaning to *mould* or *fashion*. A Sanskrit word for *body* is *deh-a* (देह) i.e. something that has been fashioned or made. And a common word for *soul* is *deh-in* (देहिन्), meaning something embodied – more analytically, something occupying a thing that has been fashioned. This word for *soul* occurs in *Śvetāśvatara Upaniṣad* 2.14:

यथैव   बम्बिं   मृद्योपलिप्तं
yathaiva bimbaṃ mṛdayopaliptam
As   a mirror with dirt smeared

तेजोमयं   भ्राजते   तत्सुधान्तम्
tejomayaṃ bhrājate tatsudhāntam
brightly   shines when well cleaned

तद्वात्मतत्त्वं   प्रसमीक्ष्य   देही
tadvātmatattvam   prasamīkṣya   dehī
so too the true self having seen the embodied (self)

एकः   कृतार्थो   भवते   वीतशोकः
ekaḥ   kṛtārtho   bhavate   vītaśokaḥ.
one, it's goal-achieved becomes freed from sorrow.

The original root for these words of kneading and fashioning is

71

something like *dheigh*. Let's take a closer look at this and the sinuous branches thence extending, before returning to ladies and lords. The final sound -*gh* is pronounced rather unpredictably in English. Witness tou*gh*, throu*gh*, do*gh*andler. It is the last of these which is found in *dheigh*. Likewise the initial *dh* is enunciated as the combination in Ma*d* *H*atter. Herein is one of the crucial clues to the links between a vast range of words across so many Indo-European languages.

Proto-Indo-European had forms of consonants that are quite recognisable in modern English – such as *b*, *p*, *t* and *d*. It also had the same range again, but where each sound was followed by a breathing, an aspiration. This occurs in modern English but generally only in compounds like *doghandler*. We can begin a word with *ph-*, like the Greek *phlegm* (φλέγμα), but we pronounce it as *f-*, not like the –*ph-* in cu*ph*older. Few languages fully maintained these aspirated consonants, but Indian languages provide some exceptions. These sounds occurred in Sanskrit, and they are still found in Urdu and Bengali among others.

For example, the Sanskrit word for fruit is *phala* (फल), and the Urdu form is *phal* (پھل).The sounds *bh* and *dh*, however, changed markedly in the languages west of India, and in the Romance languages such as Latin they both tended to become *f* (as noted in 2.2. and 2.9) .

Note from our earlier examples that the final –*gh* of *dheigh* changed too. It became a blunted *g* in the Anglo-Saxon word *hlāfdige* and it does the same in Latin. Here, the combination of the initial sound of *dheigh* changing to *f*, and the final sound becoming *g* produces a root *fig-*. This is the basis for the word *fig-ure* i.e. a model, a representation, something created. When followed by certain suffixes, *fig-* becomes *fic-* which gives us *fic-tion*. Greek dispenses with voicing, so *gh* hardens to the letter *khi* (χ), which has an aspiration like the initial sound in *c*ool rather than the final sound in ba*ck*. This way our primordial root *dheigh* spawns the Greek word *teikh-os* (τεῖχος), meaning *wall* (something that is constructed).

In every sense *dheigh* is a productive little utterance. It is easy to see how from its basic sense of *make* it is extended to things that are made, like Latin figures, Indian bodies, English dough and – as with the Greek *teikhos* – walls. We have seen that the Sanskrit root is *dih-*. In the closely related ancient east Iranian dialect of Avestan, in which are written the sacred texts of Zoroastrianism, the sound *h* becomes *z*, changing our root to *daez-*. Adding the Iranian form of the common Indo-European prefix *peri-* meaning around (as in *peri-meter*, *peri-scope* and so on) we get *pairi-daez-a*. This essentially means a *place with a wall* (something fashioned) *around it*. It is this form that entered

Greek as *para-deisos* (παρά-δεισος) and became the English *para-dise*. If it had been a genuinely Greek word we might now call it by the rather more cacophonous term **para-teike* instead. Either way we have the basic sense of a *garden* and thus *paradeisos* is the term used in *Genesis* 2.8 for the Garden of Eden:

καὶ ἐφύτευσεν κύριος ὁ θεὸς **παράδεισον** ἐν εδεμ κατὰ
kai ephuteusen kurios ho theos **paradeison** en edem kata
And planted the Lord God a garden in Eden

ἀνατολὰς καὶ ἔθετο ἐκεῖ τὸν ἄνθρωπον ὅν ἔπλασεν.
anatolas kai etheto ekei ton anthrōpon hon eplasen.
eastwards and placed there the man whom he had formed.

The same phonological mutation of original *dh* to Latin *f* is seen elsewhere. Coincidentally it occurs in another pair of gender-denoting words. A lord is a male, and a lady is a female. What then, about the *fe-* of *fe-male*? Firstly let's deconstruct *male*. It is not the same word in *male* and *fe-male*, and this is illustrated by two words related to them, *masculine* and *feminine*. *Male* derives from Latin *mas*, and our form entered the language via the Old French *masle*. The diminutive of *mas* is *mas-culus*, using the same suffix as *homun-culus*. But the *male* in fe*male* is completely different. The Latin *femina* meaning *woman* also has a diminutive form *femella* which uses a slightly different form of the same suffix. It is this word that became *female* in English. We are spelling it wrongly because *–mella* sounds a bit like *male* and both words denote gender. These things are mere coincidence. There is no real link between the words.

We have seen that *lady* isn linked to food. *Female* is quite similar. The *fe-* is from the ancient verbal root *dhe*, and as with **dheigh* and *fig-* the aspirated *dh-* becomes *f-*. This root means to *suck*. A female is one who gives suck, in the child-nourishing sense. The Latin verb *fe-lare*, cognate with the noun *fe-mina*, supplies English with the word *fe-llatio*.

The diminutive suffix is used again in another word with links to womanhood. Next time you are choosing ice cream you might go for the *small vagina* flavour, which is what *vanilla* means. The Spanish spelling *vain-illa* gives a clue to the origin. The Latin word for a *sheath* is *vagin-a*, and by adding the diminutive suffix we get **vagin-illa*, which surrenders its *g* to the mouth of a saucy Spaniard. (The same process accounts for *frail*, which is simply *fragil-e* without the *g*.) The connection between *vagin-a* and *van-illa* is apparently that the latter grows in a pod, a sort of small sheath.

2.8

Burning

Computers **and** *purgatory.*

Some time ago, a slightly alarming trend appeared to be appearing with a certain type of laptop computer with a propensity to combustion. After seeing photographs of a few potentially thigh-scorching instances, I resolved to keep my laptop well away from my lap and, where possible, only to use it in well-refrigerated circumstances. However, when we analyse the word *computer*, we find it less remarkable that the machines should burst into flames.

There are three parts to the word *com-put-er*. The first is the common prefix *com-/con-* which has an essential meaning of *together*, as in *con-cert*, *con-fuse* and so forth. The third is the agentive suffix *-er* as in *teach-er* and *farm-er*, and indicates the person or thing that does the action denoted by the preceding stem. The central element is the root of the Latin verb *put-are*, meaning *calculate* or *value*. (In fact the English word *count* is the same as *com-pute*, but entered the language via Old French which had softened the pronunciation and hence affected the spelling, whereas *com-pute* retained its harder Latin form. Compare the modern French verb *compt-er*, which stands halfway between *com-pute* and *count*). However, *put-are* has a primary meaning of *make clear*.

This root, less final consonant, crops up in Sanskrit as *pū* (पू) meaning *pur-ify* or *clarify*, and indeed the English *pure* derives from the Latin adjective *pur-us*. Nothing *pur-ifies* like *fire*, according to Saint Paul, who writes in his first letter to the Corinthians that everyone's works will be computed:

ὅτι   ἐν **πυρὶ** ἀποκαλύπτεται·καὶ ἑκάστου τὸ ἔργον
hoti   en **puri** apokaluptetai; kai hekastou to ergon
because by fire   it is revealed; and of each the work

ὁποῖόν   ἐστιν τὸ **πῦρ** δοκιμάσει.
hopoion   estin to **pur** dokimasei.
of what kind it is the fire will test.

74

The bold words in the Greek are the words for *fire*, and you will notice that they look very similar to our Latinate words for *pure*. In fact, they are from the same root. The same word *pur (πῦρ)*, when Germanicised, becomes the Old English *fŷr* and the modern *fire*, and also occurs in English as a more faithfully Hellenic *pyre* and its *pyro-technic* derivatives.

I haven't brought Saint Paul into this just to make a gratuitous biblical reference. The *pur-ifying fire* that he refers to became the basis for the concept of the pre-judgmental stage after death, which is, of course, *pur-gatory*, where sins are *pur-ged*. This is a compound of the Latin adjective *purus* and verb *agere*, a phenomenally productive root with several meanings including *drive*, *make* and *cause* (see 2.11). It occurs in several languages and features in words such as *ac-tor*, *ag-ent*, *agri-culture* and na*vig*ate (literally to drive [*ig*- is a weakened form of *ag*-] a boat [*nav-is*]). Technophobes will probably consider it apt that the words *com-puter* and *pur-gatory* are related.

2.9

Shining

Fate, phones and *baldness*

There is a tale of Japanese car manufacturer Toyota's little nomenclatural difficulty when it came to marketing their *MR2* sportscar in France. In French the register of the utterance – enunciated em-air-duh and uncomfortably similar to *merde*, which has exhausting connotations of a non-automotive nature - does not fit with our ideas of Gallic sophistication, nor with Toyota's estimation of its product. Japanese rival company Mitsubishi hit similar problems with their *Pajero* model, whose name means *grass* in some Spanish dialects but *wanker* in others. Personally I would snap up a product bearing a name so delightful for its puerility. It would tickle me greatly to drive around in a Lamborghini Belch.

The European carmaker SEAT long produced a small car called the *Ibiza*, reflecting the Spanish origins of the company. It was an honest little car. Now and then, as motor manufacturers do, the company produced what they optimistically called a "special edition" of the model. This usually involved putting differently coloured floormats in and writing a silly name on the bootlid – something innocuously, vacuously irrelevant and bubbly like *Jazz* or *Party*. I saw one example of such exotica in a car park once, and having peered in curiously at the remarkable floormats, which made the standard car seem so bland in comparison, I looked at the name on the bootlid. In what can only have been an ironic attempt to tempt thrillseekers to buy their cars, the company had called this the SEAT Ibiza *Impact*.

Impact? Why not the SEAT Ibiza *Pile-up*, or the *Hit and Run*, or the *Write-off*? It was as though the company had hired a marketing agency to think of a name for a product, but forgotten to tell them it was for a car. What would the news headlines be if the car turned out to be unsafe in some way? "Owners say *Impact* was accident waiting to happen."

SEAT's parent company Volkswagen, too, are darkly enthusiastic about associating their cars with crashes. Their luxurious saloon car the *Phaeton* is named after the worst driver in classical mythology. There are a few versions of the story, but they are characterised by his enthusiasm for driving the chariot of the sun outweighing his ability to do so, and his violent death at the hands of Zeus who had to finish him off with a thunderbolt lest his imminent collision with Earth prove apocalyptic. Why must it all be so complex? I would be happy just burbling around in my Bentley Flying Parp.

Rolls Royce, who had long ago dabbled with the name *Phaeton*, was on firmer ground with its choice of the name *Phantom*, even if the two words are clearly related. The former, as we have seen, is associated with the sun, and the latter more with something we might expect to see at night but they both share an essential sense of visibility. This is traceable back to Proto-Indo-European root *bha*. Sanskrit retains its original form and meaning quite faithfully, where it means *shine*. In Greek the initial sound is slightly altered to the *ph-* seen in our car names. But, like impetuous young Phaeton we are getting ahead of ourselves. There is more to it than that.

The basic root *bha* turns up in Greek as *phe-mi* (φη-μί) meaning *I speak* (through the same process described in 2.2 which connects *be* and *phy-sical*), whence *pho-ne* meaning *voice* and *sound*. It also shows up in Latin as *fa-ri* (*speak*) whence *fa-ma* (*rumour*) > English *fa-me*, *fa-bula* (*story*) > English *fa-bulous*, and *fa-tum* > *fa-te* (something that is spoken i.e. determined by the gods). So we see a common notion of making something apparent, either visibly or audibly. There also arises the Greek verb *phan-ein* (φαίν-ειν) meaning *shine* and a causative *phan-tazein* (φαν-τάζει), *cause to show* or *display*, whence our word *phan-tom*, a doublet of *phan-tasm*, which occurs in *Matthew* 14.26:

οἱ δὲ μαθηταὶ ἰδόντες αὐτὸν ἐπὶ τῆς θαλάσσης περιπατοῦντα
hoi de mathētai idontes auton epi tēs thalassēs peripatounta
But the disciples saw   him   on the lake   walking about

ἐταράχθησαν   λέγοντες ὅτι **φάντασμά** ἐστιν, καὶ ἀπὸ τοῦ
etarakhthēsan   legontes hoti **phantasma** estin, kai apo tou
and were troubled, saying,   "It's a ghost!",   and from

φόβου ἔκραξαν.
phobou ekraxan.
fear they cried out.

and, of course, *fan-tasy* and its slightly abbreviated doublet *fancy*.

Phae-ton, however, which only occurs as the name of our taxi driver of the apocalypse, comes from another Greek derivative *phaw-os*

77

($\phi\acute{\alpha}$ϝ-$o\varsigma$) which also yields the word *pho-to*. With this glowing list of words, it will come as little surprise that the Greek word for *white* is *phal-ios* ($\phi\acute{\alpha}\lambda$-$\iota o\varsigma$). But this comes from yet another derivative, Indo-Aryan *bhal*. And that travelled west into Old English and Gaelic to provide adjectives from a stem *bal-* or *ban-* used with reference to horses to describe white spots on the head. Thence developed the idea of a shiny or hairless head, as used here in the Middle English allegory *Piers the Plowman*. This example is from the eighth vision, where old age has been sent to remind men of death:

And Elde anone   after me and over myne heed ȝede
And Age at once (went) after me and over   my head ran

*And made me **balled** bifore   and bare on the croune.*
And made me **bald** at the front and bare on the crown.

Bald may aptly describe many owners of *fantastic Phantoms* and *fabulous Phaetons*.

2.10

Hiding

Hell and *eucalyptus trees*

Ogygia - what a perfectly splendid name for an island, or indeed any-thing. The place where the primal epic hero Odysseus was stranded for seven years on his return from Troy, hostage of the nymph Calypso, daughter of Atlas, who so very much desired to keep hold of him. It is said that, "Worse things happen at sea", but if being detained at length by a nymph with her own island is what can happen at sea, I should say that worse things probably happen on land. If you go to the Mediterra-nean island of Gozo, said to be the original Ogygia, you can stand atop Calypso's cave, the very cave where Homer placed his wayward pro-tagonist. At least, so say the Gozitos, and I wouldn't have Odysseus anywhere else. Nor, for that matter, did Calypso.

But why Calypso, and not Audrey or Doris or Octavia or Britney? There is a Greek verb *kalupt-ein (καλύπτ-ειν)* which means *cover* or *conceal*. That is what the covetous nymph *Kalup-so* did. She concealed Odysseus and kept him captive. If we isolate the root *kal-* and compare it to its Latin form *cĕl-*, we begin to see how the beguiling Calypso nymphed into English. The hard *k/c* becomes *h* in the Old English *hel-* (see 1.2), but the form that endures in English is the later Latinate im-port with prefix *con-ceal*. From the same Greek root comes the botani-cal term *cal-yx (κάλ-υξ)*, which is the protective cover around a flower in bud. *Eu-cal-yptus* (the positive prefix *eu-*, as in *eu-logy* and my un-cle's name *Eu-gene*) thus means *well-covered* in reference to that plant's capped flower. From the Latin we get *cell* and *cellar*, both covered places.

The opposite of a *eu-cal-yptus* would be something that had under-gone an *apo-cal-ypse (ἀπο-κάλ-υψις)*. The Greek preposition *apo* is a relative of the English *off*, and the appropriately final book of the Bible is the Book of *Apo-cal-ypse*, the *uncovering*, the *revealing*, the *Revela-tion*.

The original Germanic form of the verbal root occurs in the Gothic infinitive *hal-jan*. The *-j-* of the Gothic infinitival suffix, pronounced *y*, raised the root vowel from *a* to *e* by i-umlaut (see 1.3 and 1.4) before disappearing itself and leaving the Old English *hel-an* (by *hal-jan* > **hel-jan* > *hel-an*). Though this has yielded to *conceal* as a verb for hiding, it has still produced some common derivatives. What is a *hel-met* if not a cover? And if Odysseus was pained at a mere seven years of *con-ceal-ment* at the hands of *Cal-ypso*, at least he escaped the place of permanent consignment - the abode of the dead, of eternal hiding, the Gothic *hal-ja*, the English *hell*.

A similar-looking root had the inverse sense of making prominent. Its Latin form was *cel-* (contrast the *hide* verb's long vowel, *cēl-*) and this produced *ex-cel-lere* (to surpass), *cul-mināre* (to *cul-minate*), and *col-lis* (seen in the Italian *sette colli di Roma*, the *seven hills of Rome*) which becomes *hill* in English by the same process that differentiates Latin *cēl-* from Old English *hel-* above.

2.11

Driving

How *exam* is related to *synagogue*, and *wheel* and *cycle* are two forms of the same word.

If there is one sound generally assumed to have been made by homo sapiens in the earliest of times, it is *ug*. The quintessential caveman grunt whose deceptive simplicity hints at the linguistic complexity the following millennia would bring. After all, he may have just said *u* or *g*. But, as his gaze fell upon a sleeping mammoth that could supply a few week's food, the caveman combined the two sounds with a fine sense of euphony to produce *ug*. "*Ug*", said he, and all around his fellow homines sapientes cooed with their suddenly unsophisticated single *u* or lone *g* sounds about this flowery new speech. Other cavepeople may have flocked from several hundred metres away to hear this soundsmith weave an epic tale with his complex new language. Think of the possibilities that grew like wild flowers from the rich soil of *ug*.

It would take a bolder man than me to link *ug* with anything in English, although a very similar and profoundly ancient syllable supplies the basis for hundreds, possibly thousands, of words in modern English. The Proto-Indo-European verbal root *ag* means to *drive*, to *urge*, to *impel*. It appears in Sanskrit as *aj-*, in Greek and Latin as *ag-*, and in Old English as *ac-*.

From the Greek verb derives the noun *ag-ōn* (ἀγ-ών) meaning an *assembly*, *contest* or *struggle*, with a sense of driving people or forces together. The combative notion spawns the nouns *ag-ōn-istēs* (ἀγ-ων-ιστής) and *ant-ag-ōn-istēs* (ἀντ-ἀγ-ων-ιστής, with a truncated form of the prefix *anti-*), meaning *rival*, or *one who struggles*, as in the title of Milton's poem *Samson Agonistes*. A *prot-ag-onist* is the chief struggler, and the struggle itself may be *ag-ony*. (The latter word has connotations of the meaning in English where the primal root supplies the word *ache*.) A reduplicated form of the root appears in:

dem-agog-ue (δημ-αγωγ-ός), an urger of people (Greek *dēmos* [δῆμος]) i.e a leader *ped-agog-ue* (παιδ-αγωγ-ός), a leader of children (Greek *pais* [παῖς]from a stem *paid-*) i.e. a teacher

syn-agog-ue (συν-αγωγ-ή), a place where people are drawn together (The Greek prefix *syn-* is more accurately transcribed *sun-* and corresponds to the Latin *con-* or *cum-* and the Sanskrit *sam-* meaning *together*.)

It is not only people who come together in *synagogues*. *Genesis* 1.9 contains examples of both the non-reduplicated verbal and reduplicated nominal forms from *synag-* :

καὶ εἶπεν ὁ θεός   **συναχθήτω**   τὸ ὕδωρ
kai eipen ho theos **sunakhthētō**   *to hudōr*
Then God said,   "Let be gathered up the waters

τὸ ὑποκάτω τοῦ οὐρανοῦ εἰς **συναγωγὴν** μίαν
to hupokatō tou ouranou eis **sunagōgēn** *mian*
under   the heavens   in one place

In the first, the *g* (γ) of *ag* has been hardened to *kh* (χ) by the following aspirate *th* (θ). The Latin equivalent of the Greek *syn-ag-* is *co-ag-* (from **cum-ag-* which appears in Sanskrit as *sam-āj* – समाज़ - a common word for *community* in several modern South Asian languages) as in *coag-ulate*. A less elegant rendering of the verse might be, "So God said, 'coagulate the groundwater in a synagogue'".

The Latin verb's present participle is *ag-ens* (from a fuller form *ag-ents*) which comes to mean someone who causes or does, such as an *ag-ent* or *ac-tor*. An *ac-tive* person may be described as *ag-ile*, and to do something repeatedly is to *ag-itate*, which comes from the frequentative form of the Latin verb. An *ac-t* is therefore something that is done, and the prefix *ex-* gives the verb *ex-act* which can mean to *drive out*, but more often means to *weigh out*. Hence the adjective in English of the same form is used for something that has been weighed out carefully. Continuing this sense, the elements *ex-ag-men* contract to *ex-a-men-* giving the English *ex-a-mine*. Other prefixes provide the words *trans-act*, *re-act* and so forth. Surrounding elements can weaken the vowel of *ag-* to produce *ig-*. This crops up in *nav-ig-ate* (to drive a boat), *prod-ig-al* (where *prod-* is an early form of *pro-* and the literal sense of *driving forth* changes to *wasteful*), and *amb-ig-uous* (driving

82

around i.e. vague).

A notion of *driving* livestock (such as a goat, which is an *aj-ā* - अजा - in Sanskrit) or perhaps *chasing* wild animals points to the Old English word *æc-er* meaning *field*, corresponding to the Gothic *ak-rs*, the Greek *ag-ros* (ἀγ-ρός) and the Latin *ag-er*. Notice how the voiced *g* becomes an unvoiced *k* in English and Gothic due to the first Germanic consonant shift. This develops into the modern English *ac-re*, the spelling of whose suffix is influenced by the Old French which would have crept in with the Normans. If we take the Old English suffix that appears in the word wood-*en* (meaning *of wood*), and add it to our word for field we get **æc-eren* (meaning *of the field*). Say it quickly and it becomes *ac-orn*, the coda of Lysander's assault on Hermia in A Midsummer Night's Dream, whose only fault is being a bit short:

> Get you gone, you dwarf;
> You minimus, of hind'ring knot-weed made;
> You bead, you acorn.

The harvesting of the fruits of the field also uses our root. *Agri*-culture, the cultivation of the *ager*, is generally done using a tractor, which has *wheels*. Old English words did not start with *wh*- but with *hw*-. This can still be discerned in some English dialects, particularly in Scotland, in the pronunciation of words such as *what*, when the initial sound is not the *w* but the aspirate *h*, reflecting the Old English spelling *hwæt*. So, the Old English word for *wheel* was *hwēol*. However, this was a shortened form of **hweo-wol*, which answers to a Proto-Indo-European **qe-qlo*, a reduplicated form of **q^Wel* (which means *drive*, *go round*, *be in motion*. The sequence is:

**qe-qlo   <   *hweo-wol   <   hwēol   <   wheel

This **qe-qlo* goes into Greek as *ku-klo-s* (χύ-χλο-ς) and is carried back into English as *cy-cle*, which is therefore essentially the same word as *wheel*. The Sanskrit form of *ku-klo* is *cha-kra* (चक्र). We know that *cha-kra* is the same reduplicated form as *ku-klo* because in Sanskrit the velar sound *k* is palatalised to *ch* in reduplicated syllables. This term is widely used in certain spiritual theories to refer to an energy centre in the body depicted as a wheel. The Latin form of ** q^Wel* is *col*- which appears as *col-ere* meaning to *till*. This extends to be applied to an area which is tilled, which explains the Latin *in-col-a* meaning a dweller in a *col-ony*, which is a place that is tilled and therefore fit for habitation and farming. The past participle of *col-ere* is *cul-tus* which supplies the *cul-ture* in *agri-cul-ture*.

So, the Latin-based word *agri-cul-ture* actually contains two roots, *ag-* and *col-*, which both have an essential sense of *drive*. It is the driving of a driven place.

PART THREE

Nature

Roots are the fundamental units of meaning on which English is built. However, not all words are traceable to roots. In some cases there may not have ever been an action-denoting root such as that underpinning *stand* or *make*. Names of animals may simply be imitations of the sounds those animals make. In other cases, an ancient verb may have disappeared but a noun or nouns derived from it have flourished. Some things acquire names simply because of their physical resemblance to something else. In yet other cases, words may have randomly attracted affixes from completely unrelated languages and thus simple forms can become very odd-looking. In these instances we may not be able to always look to our inventory of roots, but there is an obvious alternative – agriculture and the natural world. Since the Industrial Revolution English speakers have started to loosen their links with the land. Yet, man's relationships with plants, animals, and the elements have always provided a fertile field for the cultivation and expansion of the lexicon.

3.1

Water

How *isle* and *island* are not related, but *vodka* and *otter* are.

"Nor would we deign him burial of his men till he disbursed at Saint Colme's inch ten thousand dollars to our general use", reports Ross in *MacBeth* as he tells of the routing at Fife of the Norwegian invader Sweno. Who is this Colme, and why had he an inch that served as an international financial hub? Why so small? Surely a few metres would have been better?

Saint Colme is Saint Columba, the seventh century Irish missionary who saw off the Loch Ness monster by manfully encouraging a gullible local to swim in the menaced waters having promised – apparently not entirely to the terrified swimmer's satisfaction - divine protection. His inch is the island of Inchcolm in the Firth of Forth. Actually, Columba stretched to a few inches, including Iona where he founded the religious community that endures to this day. The Bard uses this word *inch* which is very like the Scots Gaelic *innis*, found in the island's Gaelic name *Innis Choluim* whence *Inchcolm*. *Innis* is cognate with the Latin *insula* which provides the Italian *isola* (and the Latin verb *insulare* yields *insulate* and *isolate*, both of which have a sense of *detach*) and French *île*. The circumflex over the initial vowel in the French word identifies it with our anglicised form *isle*.

But we would be gravely mistaken to associate *isle* with *island*. The longer word has been infected with an *s* straying by analogy with its Latinate counterpart. For its true heritage, we must look to the Teutonic languages, where we find the German *ei-land*, Icelandic *ey-land* and other very similar forms. Clearly we have a compound whose second element is the easily recognisable *-land*. The first is an obsolete word for *water*. Old English did use the form *wæter*, of which more later, but there was also another word, *ēa*. This derived from the same source as gave Gothic *ahwa* and the Latin *aqua*. The English form of the German and Icelandic words above was *ēa-land*, but this is not the origin of *is-land*. Related to *ēa* was *īeg* or *īg* (pronounced *eeg*) which meant *a place near water*. Analogy seems to have been at work again in attaching *-land-* to *ig-* after the fashion of *ēa-land*, producing *īg-land*, whose tautologous construction then literally means *place-near-water-land*. The French influence on Middle English spelling then inserted the *s* into what had by then lost its *g* and become variously *i-lond* and *y-land*, producing *is-land*. Remnants of the original *īg* are found in place names such as *Batters-ea* (*Badric's īg*) in London and *Angles-ey* (*Ongull's īg*), the island off Wales, where the first elements are personal names.

Old English *wæter* is of similar vintage. The sound represented in English as *w* has proven quite resistant to orthographic convention in many languages. In Arabic the character for *w*, known as *waaw* (و), is also used for the vowel *u*. Many disagreements have there been on whether Julius Caesar's Latin phrase *veni, vidi, vici*, that alluringly alliterative triad of perfect tenses, ought to be enunciated more like *weni, widi, wici*. Twenty-five centuries ago, the Sanskrit grammarian Pāṇini drew attention to the interchangeable sounds *u* and *v* in rule 1.1.45 of his *Aṣṭādhyāyī*. German uses the letter *w* for the sound *v*, and the letters *v* and *f* for the sound *f*, so that the name of the car company *Volkswagen* is pronounced *Folksvagen*. The Victorian philologist W.W.Skeat - whose initials indicate a vested interest in the pronunciation of *w* – comments on the letter in the introduction to his *Etymological Dictionary of The English Language*. Referring to an orthographic amendment he had made to the Old Germanic specialist Hans Ferdinand Massmann's system for transcribing words from Gothic, he said that he had turned, "all his (Massmann's) *v*'s into *w*'s, as every good Englishman ought to do."

The following words spring from the same source as *water*. In Russian it morphs into *voda* (*вода*), which takes a diminutive suffix to form *vod-ka* (*водка*). In Sanskrit we find *udan* (उदन्), and in Greek *hudor* (ὕδωρ), which yields words like *hydr-ate* and *hydro-gen*. The polycephalous Greek aquatic beast the *Hydr-a* has an etymological relation in the monocephalous English *otter*, which gets *wet* in the *wæter*.

3.2

Cattle

Oxford is one of the most famous places in Turkey.

The name of that sweet city with its dreaming spires that nestles idylli-
cally north of England's capital, has an equally famous twin in the city
of a thousand minarets, at the heart of that most historically tumultuous
place, Istanbul. What, after all, is an *oxford*, but a place where *oxen*
may *ford*, where the beasts of the land may wade through the waters?
You don't see much of that these days in Oxford, but its name is transparent, unlike that of the River Thames which flows eastward through
the city on its way to the North Sea.

There is also a river called the Thames in India. Also flowing eastward but through the states of Madhya and Uttar Pradesh, and joining
the Ganges a little way along from that great river's confluence with the
mighty Yamuna, the *Tamsa* is the Asian twin of our insular stream. The
Tamsa takes its name from the Sanskrit word *tamas* (तमस्) meaning
darkness. Our *Thames*, which is attested in Latin as *Tamesis* and Old
English as *Temes*, is not an English word. Bear in mind that English is
not the native language round here, but a Germanic intruder. Before
English were the Celtic languages, some of which, such as Welsh and
Gaelic, are still around today. The Celtic form *Tamesas* also means
dark. Both the Sanskrit and the Celtic forms are of immense antiquity,
and it is at once extraordinary and entirely predictable that identical
names arose in distantly related languages when people separated by
thousands of miles looked into their rivers and found them a bit muddy.
But - I am meandering. Let's get back to the cattle.

We may know what an *ox-ford* is, but what is an *ox*? The Old English word is *oxa*, and the Gothic is *aúhsa*, but to illuminate the meaning
we need look east. In Sanskrit a common word for *ox* is *uksh-an* (उक्षन्),
which derives from the verbal root *uksh* (उक्ष्) meaning *sprinkle*. The
usual theory is that an *ox*, in a rudimentarily poetic sense, sprinkles a
flock of cows with its seed. An *ox*, therefore, is a sprinkler. When
something is thus sprinkled, the result is growth - of baby cows, one

would anticipate. Another form of the root *uksh* in Sanskrit is *vaksh* (वक्ष्), where the initial *u* has been strengthened into its corresponding semi-vowel *v*. This alternative root indeed has an extended sense of *grow*, and is found in Greek as *auks-(αὔξ-)*, Gothic as *wahs-*, Old English as *weax-* and Modern English as *wax*, as in, "*wax* and wane". It also occurs in Latin as the verb *aug-ere*, whence an *auc-tion* where the bids grow, and also *aug-ment* and *aux-iliary* and *au-thor* which similarly have a sense of addition or creation.

Although relatives of our word *ox* appear in Latin and Greek, as just mentioned, a different word is used in these languages for the animal itself. The Latin has *bos* and the Greek *bous (βοῦς)*. In a like manner to the Sanskrit *uksh* changing to *vaksh*, the Latin *bos* - a contraction of *bous* - changes the *u* to *v* in its main stem, giving *bov-* which is the basis of the word *bov-ine*. This basic *bo-/bou-* stem yields many useful words. There is the Greek *bu-colic (βου-κολικ-ός)* meaning rural. There are also some less immediately useful, such as the word meaning "one who is beaten with thongs made of ox hide" in this line from the Latin comedy *Mostellaria* by Plautus:

*illi   erunt   **bu**caedae   multo potius,*
(that) they will be **bull**'s hide scourged (I would) much rather,

quam   ego sim   restio.
than   I should be rope scourged.

Another Greek compound is the evocative *bou-strophēdon (βου-στροφηδόν)*. This describes an early style of writing which snaked down the page from left to right then right to left then left to right and so on, thus mimicking the turning of an ox as it ploughs a field.

In 1.6 we saw the interchange of the sounds *b* and *g* in Greek and Sanskrit which helps explain the common origin of the English words *come* and *basis*. It occurs again here and we can therefore posit the cognascence of Greek *bous* and the Sanskrit word for cow, *gaus*. This is a word of rather intricate declension in Sanskrit, and warrants its own Pāṇinian rule, *goto ṇit* (गोतो णित्, 7.1.90), which seeks to explain why the root vowel oscillates between *o* and *au*. The root of the word is taken to be *go* (गो), which occurs in words such as *Go-vinda* (गोविन्द, literally *cowherd*), one of the names of the god Kṛṣṇa. Also *go-pī* (गोपी), one of the terms for the *cowherdesses* whose loveplay with Kṛṣṇa as portrayed in the twelfth century Gīta Govinda poems has been profoundly influential in Hindu culture.

The word is found in a similar form in the ancient Iranian language of Avestan. This language is normally subdivided into Younger and Old Avestan, although there is some disagreement whether the two belong to different periods or whether they are actually contemporaneous dialects with one simply retaining more ancient features than the other. In light of this, Old Avestan is also known as Gathic Avestan in reference to the *Gathas*, or hymns, of Zarathustra which form an important part of the sacred texts of the Zoroastrian faith. The small quantity of literature in Avestan – compared to something like Sanskrit – presents a plethora of philological problems. One of the most intriguing *Gathas* is *Yasna* 29, known as the *Lament of the Cow*, in which a cow appeals to its creator to be guided from its sorrowful existence. Our Indo-Iranian *cow* word appears in the opening line:

xšmaibyā **gəuš** *urvā gərəždā...*
To you the **cow's** soul lamented...

This *bous/gaus* is a Methusaleh among words, since cattle have been essential features of agriculture for thousands of years. The association of cattle with the earth which they help to cultivate is shown in a secondary meaning of the Sanskrit word. *Go* is used sometimes to refer to the *earth* itself, and we also find this sneaking into Greek as *gē (γῆ)* with the same meaning. From this Greek comes the prefix *geo-*, as in *geo-graphy* and *geo-logy* which we use to refer to (literally) *writing about the earth* and *talking about the earth*, or more conventionally the *study of the earth* and the *study of rock*. An alternative form of *gē* is *gaia (γαîα)*, the name of a very ancient earth goddess in Greek mythology.

If we compound our word *gē* with a derivative of the root *gen* (meaning *gen-erate* or *beget* and analysed further in 2.6) we have *gē-gen-ēs (γη-γεν-ής)* – *begotten of the earth*, or *sons of the earth*. Hesiod's Theogony records that there were three giant sons of the earth goddess *Gaia* and the sky god *Uranus,* each with but one eye and called a *Cyclōps (Κύκλωψ)*, or *Round-Eye*. Perhaps the most famous – although not one of the original ones – is *Polyphēmus (Πολύφημυς)*, or *Much-Spoken-Of* or *Everywhere-Famed*, who gobbles up Odysseus' men in book nine of the Odyssey (see 2.4 for the link between *phem-* and *fame*). Related to *gē-gen-ēs* is the stem *gi-gan-t-* whence *gi-gan-tic gi-ants* who are basically *born of the earth*. This word appears in Genesis 6.4, which tells of the troubles that led to the flood and the story of Noah's Ark:

οἱ δὲ γίγαντες ἦσαν ἐπὶ τῆς γῆς ἐν ταῖς ἡμέραις ἐκείναις καὶ
hoi de gigantes ēsan epi tēs gēs en tais hēmerais ekeinais kai
There were **giants**   on the **earth** in those days,   and

μετ' ἐκεῖνο ὡς ἂν εἰσεπορεύοντο οἱ υἱοὶ τοῦ θεοῦ πρὸς τὰς
met' ekeino hōs an eiseporeuonto hoi huioi tou theou pros tas
also afterward, when the   sons of God came into the

θυγατέρας τῶν ἀνθρώπων καὶ   ἐγεννῶσαν.
thugateras tōn anthrōpōn kai   egennōsan.
daughters of   men   and they bore children to them.

ἑαυτοῖς ἐκεῖνοι ἦσαν οἱ γίγαντες οἱ ἀπ' αἰῶνος οἱ ἄνθρωποι
*eautois ekeinoi ēsan hoi **gigantes** hoi ap' aiōnos hoi anthropoi*
Those were the   **mighty men**   of old,   men

οἱ ὀνομασοί.
hoi onomasoi.
of renown.

It ought to come as no surprise that the English word *cow* is also sprung from the same fertile ground as all the above – *geo-*, *bovine*, *giant* and so forth. It occurs in Russian as *korova* (*корова*), and the milky excretions of the ladybird have given it the name in Russian *bozhya korovka* (*божья коровка*) which means *god's little cow*. This designation is found in several languages including Irish and Polish.

So, we have two Indo-European words for the animal – *ox*, expressing an idea of fertilisation, and *bo* (or *ku*), expressing an idea of generation connected to the notion of a mother earth. The second element of the name *Oxford*, although it is used as a verb itself now - to *ford* a river is to cross it - was originally a noun derived from the Old English verb *faran*, which becomes *fare* in the modern language, as in *fare-well* and *pay a fare*. This verb is more frequent in modern German where it appears as *fahren*, and where the English *ford* is transformed into the potentially troublesome *fahrt* meaning journey. (As a schoolboy arriving at my German exchange partner's house, I found unlimited amusement in announcing proudly that I had had a really good *fahrt*. It was only trumped, so to speak, by the discovery that the Latin word for an old woman was *anus*.) The First Germanic Consonant Shift changed the initial *f* of *ford* and *fahrt* from an original *p*, which is found in the Latin *port*-are and French *port*-er. This latter form also occurs in Greek, where a word for a way through is *poros (πόρος)*, whence *porous* for a surface with *pores*, such as skin.

As the English *ox* and *ford* combine to make *Oxford,* so the synonymous Greek words *bous* and *poros* combine to make *Bosporus,* the stretch of water that bisects Istanbul and divides Europe and Asia.

3.3

Fruit and veg

Why *apricot* instead of *pricot*, and *aubergine* instead of *bergine*?

The spread of Islamic culture into Europe in the Middle Ages adorned western languages with an enduring selection of words pertaining to science and nature. From Spain and Portugal, which had direct contact with Arabic speakers, words such as *al-gebra* (الجبر) and *al-kali* (ىالقال) entered the scientific language of Medieval Latin. These words were then adopted by English, whose vocabulary had already been substantially Latinised by the influence of French in the period following the Norman conquest.

The Arabic particle *al* was vigorously involved in this southern European linguistic churning. It darted around as a particle would in a reactor, variously fusing with alien words, and separating from familiar ones. Thus English has ended up with both *kohl* and *al-cohol* (الكحل) from one Arabic root, and elsewhere a floating *al* fused with a Greek word to produce the English *al-chemy* alongside *chemistry*. The London square *Traf-al-gar* takes its name from the naval battle of 1805 that took place off Cape *Trafalgar* in south-western Spain. This is a reworking of the Arabic *tarf al-gharb* (طرف الغرب) which means *western cape*.

Greater subtlety, however, is at work in many of the more curious adventures of *al* and their outcomes. Take the apricot. Shakespeare has the gardener in *Richard II* say, in one of the more apocalyptic references to fruit:

Go, bind thou up yon dangling *apricocks*,
which, like unruly children, make their sire
stoop with oppression of their prodigal weight.

Shakespeare's variant spelling reflects the Spanish *al-baricoque*, which is itself a corrupted form of an Arabic *al-barquq* (البرقوق). This is used in modern Arabic to refer to plums, while the current word for *apricot* is *mishmish* (مشمش) However, *al-barquq* is not actually Arabic. It is an Arabic rendering of (possibly a Middle Greek form of) the Latin *prae-coquus*, (*pre-cocious* in modern English) meaning *early-ripe*, with the prefix *al*. The *l* disappears to form *a-pricot*. The speed of an *a-pricot*'s ripening is sufficiently notable that reference to it has not only supplanted the traditional words for the fruit, which generally referred to the places they were cultivated – *armeniaca* or *damasco*. It has also produced the Arabic phrase *filmishmish* (في‌المشمش) – *in an a-pricot's time* or *when the apricots ripen* - which can be employed to express doubt that something can be done as quickly as has been asserted. For example:

"Thank you for waiting. Your call will be answered shortly."
"Filmishmish."

So much for apricots. The history of *aubergine* is frankly ludicrous. To the European ear it connotes *auberge*, a cosy hostel in France, or *Bergen*, fresh hills in Germany. That is only because our Arabic friend *al* has attached himself to a foreign word again. *Au-bergine* is the English rendering of Arabic *al-badinjan* (الباذنجان), which comes from Persian *badimjan* (بادمجان). But the Persian appears to be based on a Sanskrit compound *vātiṃgaṇa* (वातगिण, modern Hindi *baingana*), from Sanskrit *vā* (वा, meaning *blow*), which is cognate with Russian *veter* (ветер), Latin *ventus* and English *wind*. The second element *gaṇa* derives from the verb *gam* which means *go* and is related to the English verb *come* (see 1.6). This is a very specific word in Sanskrit with no application other than to the name of this vegetable – and it basically means something that prevents flatulence. *Al* has gracefully obscured the elemental associations of this unfortunately named food. It is not only associated with physical sickness. Negative connotations are closer in its Italian name *melanzana*, a contraction of Latin *mela insana* (*bad apple*). In *Manners and Customs of the Modern Egyptians* the nineteenth century Arabist E.W.Lane notes that madness is said to be more common in Egypt when the black badingan is in season, and relates the following (unintentionally?) comical incident:

The neighbours unanimously declared that the husband was mad...One exclaimed: "There is no strength or power but in God! God restore thee!" Another said: "How sad! He really was a worthy man." A third remarked: "Badingans are very abundant just now."

3.4

Swine

Piggery-jokery.

"But that I am forbid
   To tell the secrets of my prison-house,
   I could a tale unfold, whose lightest word
   Would harrow up thy soul; freeze thy young blood;
   Make thy two eyes, like stars, start from their spheres;
   Thy knotted and combined locks to part,
   And each particular hair to stand on end,
   Like quills upon the fretful *porpentine*."

And what a tale indeed it is to which Hamlet's father alludes, of inter-necine noble-nobbling and hardly less heartless extra-conjugal jiggery-pokery. The quills upon the back of the pint-sized pig we know as a *porcupine* provide an apt point of comparison for the horripilative effects of the horrible secrets of that dreadful spectre's demise.

Pig's backs were quite inspirational in other ways to our agricultural ancestors. The Greek word for a young pig was *choiros* (χοῖρος) and a feminine derivative *choiras* (χοιράς) was used for a low rock that rises above the sea like a hog's back. The Latin word for *pig* is *porcus*, which supplies English *pork* and the first element of *porcu-pine* (the second element being *spinus* meaning a *thorn* or *prickle*), a creature which might otherwise be called a *spiny swine*. This Latin form had a diminutive *porc-ella*, using the same suffix we saw in an earlier section in the formation of the word *female* (from *femella*) and *vanilla* (from *vaginilla*). The word *porc-ela-in* comes from *porc-ella*. The link is that a type of shell with a shiny, ridged surface, the *porc-ellana*, and the sheen on what became known as *porc-elain* was considered rather similar. The shell itself was called *porc-ella* because its ridges resembled a sow's vulva. In case you suspect at this point that we are drifting into the realm of etymological fancy, I call as witness in support of this ludicrousness one of Ancient Rome's leading agricultural experts, Marcus Terentius Varro, who also happened to be a philologist. In his *Res Rusticae* (*Country Matters*) he discusses the tradition of sacrificing a pig on various occasions including weddings, and notes rather playfully the lexical connection between little pigs and brides:

nostrae mulieres, maxime nutrices, naturam qua feminae sunt in
our   women, especially nurses, the mark   of the sex

*virginibus appellant **porcum**, et graecae **choeron**...*
in girls   they call **porcus**, and the Greeks **choiros**...

This indicates that the association of the two was well-established by the first century B.C. when Varro was writing.

We saw in 2.7 that *vanilla* means *small vagina*, so if you find yourself eating vanilla ice cream from a porcelain dish you are, from a philological perspective, being gynaecologically overwhelmed.

The Latin form also supplies the *por-* in *por-poise*, which is a compound of *porcus* and *piscis* meaning *pig-fish*. French and German employ terms based on the Latin adjective *suinus* (pertaining to *swine*) – *mar-souin* and *Meer-schwein*, meaning *sea-pig*. That Latin adjective derives from the noun *sus* which reflects the English *sow*. The Greek rendering of this word replaces the initial sibilant with aspirate to make *hus* (ὗς). The aforementioned Varro writes of pig sacrifice and goes on to wrongly derive the name of the animal from the verb *thu-ein* (θύ-ειν) meaning *sacrifice*, which is not unreasonable given the context but philologically inadmissible. The Greek is seen in the biblical commandment not to eat pork, which first occurs in *Leviticus* 11.7:

καὶ τὸν **ὗν**.........ἀκάθαρτον τοῦτο ὑμῖν
kai ton **hun**.......akatharton touto humin
And the **swine**...is unclean   to you

Whereas Latin's porky form makes its way into *Matthew* 7.6:

nolite dare   sanctum canibus: neque mittatis
Do not give what is holy to the dogs: nor   cast

*margaritas vestras ante **porcos**.*
your pearls   before swine.

PART FOUR

Etcetera

So far we have looked at some of the processes of change which have distinguished English from other languages. We have seen sounds and forms evolve in supremely logical ways, and we have seen how apparent irregularities are often better perceived as additional manifestations of regularity. However, as with other evolutionary processes, though some changes are immense we can also observe that other things hardly change at all. Alternatives may emerge which render the original superfluous, but rather than the new replacing the old we find sometimes several ways of saying the same thing. This is true not only for individual words but for features of syntax and morphology too. Some things just resist and persist. This section looks at a few of those things.

4.1

Numbers

Who made *one* and *once* the only words in English that start with *o* but sound like they start with *w*?

We have so far met with many examples of words which superficially seem unrelated, but can be linked through stages of sound change. Less cryptically, some of the most obviously related words in Indo-European languages include words for family members – *father*, *vater* (German), *pater* (Latin), *pitṛ* (Sanskrit पितृ) – and numbers. Indeed for quite some period of philological study a common way of subgrouping languages within the Indo-European family was on the basis of how the word for 100 was pronounced. We shall shortly look at numbers one and two. First, what's a number?

The word *num-ber* derives from a root *nem-* meaning *allot* or *share*. It occurs in this form in Greek where it yields the name of the goddess of retribution *Nem-esis* (Νέμ-εσις), who deals out direness to deviants. Some Latin derivatives retain the original *e* vowel but most use the variant with *u* which underlies modern European words such as *num-ber* (and its French counterpart *nom-bre*), *num-eral* and so forth. The original *e* remains, however, in the form of this important verb which, though it has faded rather from modern English, survives in other Germanic languages where the meaning shifted from giving to taking. Modern German has it as *nehm-en*, which comes from a Germanic form *nim-*.

Here is an example in Old English (in this case the pastparticiple) from *Beowulf*, occurring in a story told during the feast to mark the hero's defeat of the monstrous Grendel. The story is of the funeral of Hildeburh's kin, including her husband Finn, king of the East Frisians, who are killed fighting the Danes. There are some outstandingly gruesome images of their slaughter and equally so of their cremation, which sees bursting wounds and melting heads. This is the aftermath of the killing itself:

Þā wæs heal roden
Then was the hall decorated

fēonda fēorum,   *swilce Fin slægen,*
with the foes' lives,   so too (was) Finn slain,

cyning   on corþe,   *ond sēo cwēn* **numen**.
the king with his troop,   and the queen taken.

We meet the verb's third person plural preterite in Old English's sister language Gothic in *Matthew* 6.2, when Jesus says that hypocrites boast of their charitable deeds only to seek praise from men:

amēn   qiþa izwis: **andnēmun** *mizdōn seina*
Verily I say to you; they have received their reward.

The Old English form of the word *one* – *ān* - is the source of the indefinite article – *a* or *an* (as in French its cognate number *un* serves as the indefinite article). The numeral occurs twice in *Matthew* 25.15 in the story of the venture capitalist who funded three start-ups:

And **ānum** *hē sealde fīf pund,*   *sumum twā,*   *sumum* **ān**.
And to one he gave five pounds, to another two, to another one.

We have seen several examples of Old English *ā* being rounded to an *o* sound (*stān* to *stone* and so on), and this accounts also for the Old English *ān* (meaning the number 1) becoming *one*. This change occurred when the vowel was stressed. The same *ān* also had an unstressed form retaining the original vowel, hence the parallel existence of the numeral *one* and the article *an*. Originally there was only one article, *ān*, but somewhere in the evolution of Old English into Middle English the *n* of *ān* began to fade before words beginning with consonants while being retained before vowel-initial words.

A similar process is found in Arabic in which the *l* of the definite article *al* is absorbed into certain sounds occurring initially in immediately following words, with a resultant lengthening of the initial consonant. The letters which do this are called sun letters, after the word for *sun* whose initial letter serves as an example – what is written *al shams* (الشمس) is pronounced *ash shams*. In Arabic the sound change is not reflected in spelling (there is no alternative article consisting of just *a* for use with sun letters alongside the fully enunciated *al* used before moon letters), but English has favoured two spellings to reflect the different pronunciation. In English there are also instances where a word's initial *n* has gravitated leftward to the article itself – there used to be a snake called *a nadder* – and where the *n* of the article has gone rightward to become the intial sound of the word – there was once an amphibian called *an ewt*.

Stress not only created the parallel number and article. It also caused diphthongization of the stressed vowel of the number form, which is to say that its one vowel sound became two. Old English *ān* changed to what is heard in the derivatives *on-ly*, *al-one*, and *l-one-ly*. The diphthong further mutated in an interesting innovation which appears to have taken place in the west of England about five hundred years ago. An initial *w* developed exclusively at the beginning of the words *one* and *on-ce*, making them the only words in English beginning with *o* but pronounced as though they begin with *w*. The *w* innovation is quite an oddity, although it is interesting to note the entirely coincidental similar development English made with related Romance forms based on Latin *un-us*. In French and Italian this is pronounced as vowel-initial (i.e. French *une* sounds like *oon*, and Italian *uno* sounds like *oono*) but loanwords in English have acquired an invisible *y* which creeps into the pronunciation of things such as *unique* and *university*. This was one of several developments of the long *ū* sound between Middle and Modern English, and of course means that we use the *a* form of the article rather than *an* with these words.

As we have two forms of the indefinite article in English for euphonic reasons, so French has two forms of the indefinite article to indicate either masculine or feminine nouns – *un* for masculine and *une* for feminine. No other numerals in French require gender agreement. However, ancient Indo-European languages usually declined the first three or four numerals for gender - masculine, feminine, and neuter - and also case -nominative, accusative, genitive etc. This meant that fully declining *one* (*eka* एक) in Sanskrit, which has eight cases and three genders, required twenty-four forms, although in reality seven of the eight forms were identical in the masculine and the neuter. Sanskrit is unusually thorough in treating all numbers as declinable – basically as adjectives - whereas Greek is more typical in only declining 1 to 4. Old English mostly limited declension to 1 to 3, and there is a legacy of this in the modern language.

The masculine form for 2, *twēgen*, is most faithfully reflected in the archaic *twain*. The feminine and neuter shared the form *twā* which has become *two*. The preposition *be-tween* appears to follow the masculine, but it is actually a compound of the preposition *be* (elsewhere spelt *by*) and a contracted dative form (the preposition *be* requires the dative case) of the adjective *twēon*, derived from the basic word for the numeral, hence its use to mean *by two things*. We find it in the Old English poem *Exodus*:

*ac   hīe gesittaþ **be sǽm twēonum**   oþ Ēgipte incaþēode.*
and they shall settle **by** the **two** seas as far as the nation of Egypt

This stock phrase *be sǽm twēonum* also occurs several times in Bēowulf, where it may have referred to the North and Baltic Seas, or carried a more general meaning of *everywhere*. The same adjective occurs in Gothic in *Mark* 7.31:

*kwam   at marein Galeilaiē mith **tweihnáim** markōm*
He came to the sea of Galilee amid the **two**   boundaries of

Daíkapaúlaios.
Dekapolis.

In like fashion German derives its preposition *zwi-schen* from its number *zwei*. (The initial *z*, representing a *ts* sound, developed from the original Germanic *t* of English and Gothic in the High Germanic Consonant Shift, also responsible for the initial *th* of *three* becoming the *d* in German *drei*).

Through the feminine/neuter form *twā* the relation to forms in other languages is clear – Gothic *twái*, Latin *duo*, Greek *duo* (δύο), Sanskrit *dvi* (द्वि). The First Germanic Consonant Shift changed the original initial *d* to *t* in English and Gothic, and the *w-v-u* interchange reflects tiny variations of one sound. At an early stage the idea of duality seems to have assumed a slightly sinister sense, although an alternative form *bi-* or *bis-* remained neutral and simply meant *two*, hence *bi-ennial* meaning *every two years*, and *bis-cuit* meaning *twice-cooked*. But its twin *di-* or *dis-* became a widely used negative or negating prefix. To *dis-cover* something is to separate it from its cover; *dis-ease* is a separation from *ease*; in *dis-aster* (from French *des-astre*) it has a wholly negative meaning - literally *bad star*, in the sense of *ill*-fated. Although the connotation with stars has now disappeared, it must have had some currency when Shakespeare used it in *Hamlet* in a passage full of likewise astrally portentous images:

As, stars with trains of fire, and dews of blood,
Disasters in the sun; and the moist star,
Upon whose influence Neptune's empire stands,
Was sick almost to doomsday with eclipse.

4.2

Repetition and Superfluidity

What's the difference between *enter* and *enter into*?

Of the streams of thought that feed into language one of the least valued brings a flow of corporate neological bastardy that encourages the use of new terms for things which are already adequately defined. I know a man who, in his professional life (and maybe other situations too), no longer just talks to people or tells them things. He *captures* information (which is presumably otherwise wild) and *escalates* it to his superiors or *cascades* it to his inferiors (*cascading on* people sounds a bit unhygienic). When I asked him what word he used to refer to communicating with people on the same level as him, it transpired that he didn't have such a word. Perhaps *ripple* or *spray*? "I was spraying to a friend this morning something I had captured while it was being cascaded to people who, frankly, have no business being cascaded to and it was really only suitable for escalation. What part of the cascade-spray-escalate framework do these people not understand?" This treatment of English is neither creative nor clever, and to call a *spade* a *biomass realignment accelerator* or a *geo-human interface manager* or a *supradigital leverage multiplier* or even a *giant spoon* merely indicates that there is probably something wrong with you.

One coining emanating from this humourless field is the noun *deliverable*. As far as I can ascertain this means a *result* in the form of a *product* or *service* or *achieved target*. Have these words ceased to resonate in modern corporate culture? Do they somehow fail to express the raw and intense vagueness of *deliverable*? One can *provide* a *service* or *make* a *product*. Certainly, there is a semantic tautology in *making* a *product;* it means the same as *produce* a *product*, which we don't say. But what does one do with a *deliverable*? And how is it to be described? "Is this deliverable deliverable?" Does anyone talk of *delivering deliverables*? If *deliverable* does not collocate with the verb *deliver*, then it follows that *deliverables* cannot be *delivered* and are therefore, by default, *undeliverable*. And how can you have an *undeliverable deliverable*? If a *deliverable* is *undeliverable*, then it is rendered logically non-existent by semantic implosion. Need we further proof that this word is not merely unnecessary but unusable?

This is by the by. It is not the only superfluous thing about English. A tautologous construction contains multiple words meaning the same thing. Tautology is found in *Lake Windermere*. (*Mere* is an Old English word for *lake*, related to *mar-ine* and identical with the first element of *mar-souin* and *meer-schwein*, the French and German words for *porpoise* given in 3.4.) Also in *Sahara Desert* (*sahra* - □اصحرا - is the Arabic word for *desert*).

A pleonastic construction contains multiple words which do not have the same meaning but convey the same idea. For example, one *enters a room*. To *enter into a room* would be a pleonasticism. But we can *enter into negotiation*. The idea of *into* already exists in the verb *enter*. The verb is an Anglicised form of the Latin compound *in-trare* which combines the directional preposition *in* with a form of the ancient verbal root **ter-*. This has a basic sense of movement. (It appears in Sanskrit as *tṝ* - तृ - and is used in the derived noun *ava-tāra* – अवतार -, something which descends. In Sanskrit this is generally used in the context of a deity descending from heaven in human form, and the word itself has since descended into computer jargon as *avatar*.) The preposition certainly seems unnecessary and pleonastic. However, there may be another explanation.

Phrasal or multi-word verbs and complex verb structures abound in English, in part because the verb forms themselves and their immediate derivatives (by which I mean participles) have been reduced to just five forms for strong verbs e.g. *drive, drives, drove, driven, driving*, and four for weak verbs e.g. *want, wants, wanted, wanting*. By contrast, the number of forms in a full verbal conjugation in Greek or Sanskrit including participles (and in the case of Vedic Sanskrit around twelve forms of the infinitive) runs into several hundred. There were a greater number of discrete forms which carried a greater range of meaning. One important function of, say, the imperfect in Greek was inceptive, which is to say an imperfect such as *epauon* (ἔπαυον) could be translated as *I began to stop*. English requires other means to express inceptivity.

One way is to use another verb, such as *begin to*, and another is to use a particle such as *into*. Conventionally *into* is a preposition, but consider *enter into negotiation*. We have established that *enter* does not need a preposition, and indeed we could as easily say *enter negotiation*. So is the role of *into* here more adverbial than prepositional? As *entering negotiation* focuses on the beginning of the action of *negotiating*, so *into* focuses on the beginning of the action of *entering* – it seems to express a more intensely inceptive sense than the basic verb-object construction itself can carry. This distinguishes the meaning from that of *enter a room*, where we may understand *enter* to mean the whole action of *entering* rather than simply the beginning of the action. Alternatively, it may simply be that *into* is entirely pleonastic when used with *enter*. Pleonasticism of particles is not implausible, but often these multi-word constructions arise from a need to merge ideas and create shades of meaning. The paucity of discrete verb forms in English has thus forced speakers to compensate with multi-word phrases some of which either contain or appear to contain redundant particles. These constitute probably the most difficult area of vocabulary for a non-native speaker to understand. The number of phrasal verbs is huge, new ones are constantly being formed, and their meaning can seem so finely nuanced as to be unnecessary. Most native speakers would struggle even to adequately explain any difference between *sit* and *sit down*.

Compensating for lack of verb forms does not merely require greater use of prepositions and adverbial particles. When we need to change the function of a word – from, say, a verb to a noun e.g *feed* to *food* – or change the tense of a verb – from, say *feed* to *fed* – we can alter the form either by changing the vowel, as in *feed food fed*, or by adding an affix – *walk / walk-ed*. This is inflection. Languages which make extensive use of inflection are known as synthetic. Apart from the above examples and one or two others, inflection has almost completely disappeared from English. It is no longer synthetic but isolating. For example, in Old English information about the mood as well as the tense of a verb can be conveyed by inflection – *wē fēden* uses two words where these days we would need three to say *we may feed*. The role of the subjunctive has been almost entirely taken by modal auxiliaries like *may* and *should*.

That this movement away from synthetic structures is not complete we can see in the paradigm of the past simple. If questions and negatives in the past simple use an auxiliary verb + infinitive construction – *Did you go? / I didn't go* – rather than the past simple of the verb – *went* – why don't we completely standardise the paradigm and say *I did go* as well? We could at a stroke dispense with all past simple forms except that of the auxiliary, which has been completely delexicalised as it is i.e. in *I didn't go* the word *did* doesn't actually mean anything. If two of the three past simple constructions already don't use the traditional preterite form, it does look rather superfluous.

As with the proliferation of phrasal verbs, this isolating tendency does not make the language any simpler. In addition to tense, further information about aspect or mood or manner which can all be expressed by a discrete verb form in a heavily inflected synthetic language such as

Sanskrit is instead conveyed in English by periphrastic constructions utilising auxiliary verbs. How about a future perfect continuous passive causative intensive? - *I will have been being caused to be tickled hard*. I am not suggesting that Sanskrit would express all this in one word, although it probably could, but the use of ten words to express a single action in English is an extreme illustration of how the erosion of inflection has generated a no less complex system of multi-word verbal constructions.

Similarly with nouns. In Sanskrit, one word - *grhāt* (गृहात्) – requires at least three words – *from a house* - in English. The Sanskrit noun appears in the dictionary as *grham*, and the ablative sense of *from* is understood from the different ending of *grhāt*. If we want to say *from the two houses* we use the ablative dual *grhābhyām* (गृहाभ्याम्). In Sanskrit and Latin words can be arranged more loosely within a sentence because the inflections illuminate the functions of the words – the subject, the direct object, the indirect object, adjectives qualifying all these and so on. There are certain rules of syntax and style but word order is generally freer than in modern English. The sentence, "Don't let the bottom fall out of your world" is understood to be an encouraging, consoling statement. If the words *world* and *bottom* change places, it sounds like a warning not to eat a hot curry. This change in meaning would not happen in Latin because the word endings would indicate what was falling out of where.

Some languages have retained much fuller systems of inflection while also establishing a fixed word order. German has four cases and Russian six but we cannot plonk words anywhere we want. In these instances the ancient case system is almost completely superfluous, which is what a young Winston Churchill thought. Running through the declension of the word for *table*, his Latin teacher explained that the vocative case would be used in addressing a table, to which the schoolboy quite reasonably protested that this was not something he was in the habit of doing. Vestiges of nominal inflection remain in English. We see it chiefly in plurals (one monkey / two monkey*s*), possessives (the monkey*'s* banana), and pronouns (*I* saw *him* / *He* saw *me*), but even these are not wholly necessary. Why do we need a plural *s* when we have numbers to specify quantity and the word *a* to show when we mean *only one*?

There are also several instances in English where a pair of words exists which are actually the same word subject to tiny modification. Some words beginning with *w* correspond exactly to others beginning with *g* – *warranty* and *guarantee* are the same word. The initial *w* reflects an original Germanic sound, whereas the initial *gu* reflects the modified French – and specifically the Parisian – pronunciation which prevailed from the Middle French period onwards (Old French also had *warantie*) and survives in the modern language as *garantie*. The same interchange accounts for the Old English-derived *w-arden* and the French-derived *gu-ardian*, and their respective verb forms. Also *w-ar* and the French *gu-erre* (as in *guerr-illa*), and *w-ise* (as in *other-wise*) and *gu-ise* (as in *dis-guise*) with the sense of *manner*.

There is also repetition on a morphological level. The suffix *–ly* used to form English adjectives and adverbs – low*ly*, slow*ly* – is a contraction of the Old English word *līc*. This originally meant *body* (as in the *Lyke Wake Walk*, the east-west crossing of the North Yorkshire Moors associated in folklore with the journey of a soul to purgatory) and came to mean *form*, so when it is appended to *heaven* to produce *heaven-ly*, we get an adjective that means *(having a form) like heaven*. Indeed, *līc* became the modern word *like*, so it would be more accurate to say that *heavenly* means *heaven-like*. The use of *–ly* as the main means of deriving adverbs, and the consequent erosion of its nominal meaning, perhaps accounts for *like-ly*, which is simply the same word used twice. This form has not emerged in German, although the same suffix - *-lich* - is used in derivation identically to the English *–ly*. Further, the German form of the Old English noun *līc* survives in the modern language as *Leiche*, which retains its bodily association and means *corpse*. So, where the Old English **līc-līc* (also attested in Old Norse as *līk-ligr*) became *like-ly* and late acquired a sense of *probable*, the same repetitious compound in German would be *leiche-lich* and mean *corpse-like*. That's one that doesn't make it onto the list of false friends in your phrasebook.

4.3

Auxiliary verbs

If *I work* and *she works*, why not *I can* and *she cans*? And where did the *l* in *could* come from?

"The whole entirely depends upon the auxiliary verbs," declares Walter Shandy in Laurence Sterne's *Life and Opinions of Tristram Shandy, Gentleman*. He argues that the imagination is freed into a universe of expressive possibilities when properly trained in the use of auxiliaries:

Didst thou ever see a white bear? Cried my father....No, an' please your honour, replied the corporal.- But thou couldst discourse about one, Trim, said my father, in case of need?- How is it possible, brother, quoth my uncle Toby, if the corporal never saw one?- 'Tis the fact I want, replied my father,- and the possibility of it is as follows.

A white bear! Very well. Have I ever seen one? Might I ever have seen one? Am I ever to see one? Ought I ever to have seen one? Or can I ever have seen one?

Would I had seen a white bear! (for how can I imagine it?)

If I should have seen a white bear, what should I say? If I should never see a white bear, what then?

If I never have, can, must, or shall see a white bear alive; have I ever seen the skin of one? Did I ever see one painted?- described? Have I never dreamed of one?

Did my father, mother, uncle, aunt, brothers or sisters ever see a white bear? What would they give? How would they behave? How would the white bear have behaved? Is he wild? Tame? Terrible? Rough? Smooth?

-Is the white bear worth seeing?-

-Is there no sin in it?-

Is it better than a black one?

Auxiliary verbs, not infrequently employed in several languages, are a particularly notable feature of English. Especially so in their assumption of many of the modal functions of the subjunctive and optative constructions in classical languages.

One primordial root *gen supplies English with both the verb *know* and the auxiliary *can*. The semantic link in English is that one *can* do something because one *knows* how to. Modern German uses the two verbs with a clear distinction:

The verb *können* gives - Ich *kann* Englisch = I *can* (speak) English

The verb *kennen* gives - Ich *kenne* ihn nicht = I do not *know* him

German also uses the verb *wiss-en* – related to words of seeing in English such as *vis-ion* and *vis-a* and examined in more detail in 2.1 - to mean *know a fact*.

Even in Old English *cunn-an* had assumed the auxiliary function which it performs today. It was one of the handful of Germanic verbs classified as a preterite present, which is to say that the form used in the present tense – for example the first person singular *ic can*, or in Gothic *ik kann*, with a different vowel from the infinitives *cunn-an* and *kunn-an* – is actually a preterite, or past tense form of a strong verb, which has come to have a present tense meaning. This had two important structural implications. The first is that *can* and all other modal verbs in modern English do not form their third person singular with *s*. We say *she works* but not *she *cans*, because in Old English the third person singular preterite was the same as the first person singular i.e. *can*. (This also accounts for the form *wot*, rather than *wots*, in the line from the Thomas Brown poem quoted in 2.1.) The second is that a new preterite was formed to express the past tense and this was formulated like the preterite of a weak verb – characterised by ending in –*d* or –*ed* - , resulting in a mixed conjugation of strong present and weak preterite forms. We know the past tense of *can* to be *could*, but how did we get there?

To reconstruct the development of *could* we need look eastward to Gothic where the preterite was *kun-þa*, equivalent to Old English *cun-þe*. In 1.1 we saw that the coastal Germanic tribe the Ingvaeones had an aversion to the sound *n* being followed by *th*, preferring to drop the *n* and lengthen the preceding vowel, as in Old English *mūþ (mouth)* beside Gothic *munþ-s*. Similarly here, the Old English dropped the *n* of *cun-þe* and lengthened the vowel to produce *cū-þe*. Much later in the sixteenth century, by analogy with the other preterite present verbs *shall* and *will*, whose preterites *shoul-d* and *woul-d* naturally included the letter *l*, *cū-þe* became *coul-d* just for appearance's sake. The *l* of *cou-ld* is then a very late addition and is a good example of the way language gravitates towards order, creating a new structure that obscures an original one. We are reminded still of the old form in the nearly obsolete adjective *un-couth*, literally meaning *unknown* or *strange,* but chiefly used these days to mean *ill-mannered.*

While *can* was carving out a career as a Germanic auxiliary, its brother cognate meaning *know* in Old English, *cnāw-en,* retained its original meaning and function as it did with remarkable regularity across the Indo-European world. Let's digress a moment from the abstractions of auxiliaries to examine it. The root *cnā-* occurs in the reduplicated Greek form *gi-gnō-skō (γι-γνώ-σκω)* and the Latin *(g)no-scere,* whence *co-gn-ition, a-gno-stic* and *i-gno-rant.* Gothic's *kunn-an* seems to have done duty to mean both *can* and *know.* Here's an example of the latter from *John* 14.7 which uses the second person plural preterite subjunctive:

Iþ   **kunþ**ē*deiþ mik, aíþþáu*   **kunþ**ē*deiþ jah*
If you had **kno**wn   me, truly you would have **kno**wn also

attan meinana.
my   father.

Even when we delve into some of the more arcane areas of Indo-European we find this root easily recognisable in both form and function. The Old Persian language of the Achaemenid Empire of the sixth to the fourth centuries BC – then the biggest empire the world had ever known – survives only in relatively few cuneiform inscriptions, the most substantial of which is on the rock of Behistun near modern Kermanshah in western Iran. This tells of the volatile events surrounding the ascent and rule of Darius the Great. The Greek historian Herodotus, not having to cope with the constraints of carving cuneiform into limestone a hundred metres up a cliff face, weaves at greater length a riotously tall version of the tale in his *Histories.* He has a woman marrying a man without realising he doesn't have any ears, and a faithful counsellor leaping to his death from a tower. Understandably Darius himself prefers to focus on other details such as his success in crushing the tiresomely common rebellions against him. In an episode of enduring historical mystery Darius the pretender hunts down the villainous Gaumāta – Herodotus' earless wonder – whom he claims has murdered Bardiya, the rightful heir to the throne, and assumed the dead man's identity. Here we see the third person plural subjunctive of the Old Persian form of our *cnā-/gnō* verb. Gaumāta is said to be slaying Bardiya's people:

110

xšnā́sātiy   tya adam   naiy Bardiya
(lest) they should **know** that I (am) not Bardiya

The cliché *to know someone in the biblical sense* does not apply to the extract from *John* 14.7 quoted above. It does, however, apply in the case of this snippet of *Matthew* 1.25 vouching for Joseph's romantic restraint around Mary before the birth of Jesus:

Old Church Slavonic - *ne   **zna**azhe yee*
Modern Russian   - *an ne **znal** yeyo* (он не **знал** её).
                  he did not **know** her

This usage corresponds to the second of the two examples given above in German, and would thus be rendered, "er **kann**te sie nicht". We see that the initial consonant has softened in the Slavic languages to a *z* sound (*zna-*) from the harder and more original gutturals in the Germanic *k* (German *kann-* and *kenn-*, Old English *cnā-* and *cunn-*, Gothic *kunn-*), and the Greek and Latin *g* (*gnō*). The Old Persian *xš* (*xšnā-*) hints at a softening which is more clearly attained in the Sanskrit form *jñā-* (ज्ञा).

Returning to auxiliaries, another very prevalent verb is the one so commonly used to refer to the future. English only has two tenses – present and past. It has only ever had two tenses. They are distinguished either by the addition of a suffix – "Today I perambulate, and yesterday I perambulate*d* - or by vowel gradation – "Today I stink, and yesterday I stank", as explained in 1.4. These two tenses have different aspects – the present *I fly*, the progressive *I am flying*, the perfective *I have flown* – and different voices – the active *I fly*, the passive *I am flown* – and different moods – the imperative *Fly!*, the subjunctive *That he fly once more is a wish we share* – but all are constructed from a two-tense system. We have ways of referring to the future – *I am flying tonight*, *I am going to fly next week*, *I shall be flying so seek me not on the earth* – but there is no future tense in the sense that there is a past tense e.g. *drive, drove*.

The Old English sentence, "Hē behorsaþ ēow" could mean, "He deprives you of horses", or "He will deprive you of horses." This is not so in many other languages. The Sanskrit *jīvati* (जीवति) for *he lives* adds the infix *–isy-* to form *jīviṣyati* (जीविष्यति) for *he will live*. The Latin *amo* (*I love*) adds the infix *–b-* to form *amabo* (*I shall love*). If, however, we were to say, "Hē wille ēow behorsian," (literally, "He will deprive you

111

of horses") the primary meaning is not that *he is going to deprive you of horses* but *he wishes to deprive you of horses*. Modern German retains this sense of volition – "Er will dich von Pferden zu berauben" means "Hē wille ēow behorsian." A desire to do something indicates that the action itself is not yet done and therefore in the future, hence the English verb *will* has mostly lost its original sense of *want* and come to be used almost exclusively as a future tense indicator.

We have seen that the past tense of *can* was originally *cūþe* and acquired the *l* seen in the modern *could* by analogy with its preterite present playmates one of which was *will*. The relationship of *will* and *would* is more transparent than that of *can* and *could*. We simply have a vowel change and the addition of the entirely regular *d* ending of the weak preterite, and this change can be seen in the following sentences in Gothic and Old English:

*Fráuja, jabái **wileis**,   magt mik gahráinjan.*
Lord, if you are willing, make me clean.
(Matthew 8.2)

*Ic Ǽlfrīc **wolde** þās lȳtlan bōc āwendan tō Engliscum gereorde*
I Ǽlfrīc wanted this little book to translate to the English language
(Introduction to his *Latin Grammar*)

The same verb occurs in Latin as *velle* which yields the words *volunteer* (someone who does something *will-ingly*) and *vol-uptuous* (given up to pleasure).

As Walter Shandy opines at the start of this section, auxiliary verbs afford an extensive range of nuance. The concept of obligation has been disinclined to settle definitively on any particular verb. *Must* is mysterious. It has but one form these days, had a fairly limited application in Old English with the sense *to be allowed*, became more prominent in Middle English and does not appear to have any cognates outside of Germanic. In Old English, obligation was expressed chiefly by *scul-an* (*sc* pronounced as *sh*), whose first person singular present *sceal* and preterite *scolde* point to the modern *shall* and *should*. There is a general notion that *will* expresses volition and *shall* indicates obligation by an external force, but in reality this does not really explain much. If the general rule holds true, how are we to account for, "You will start tomorrow", when I cannot know if that is actually what you want? It would be better to use *shall* here. Logically I should mostly only be able to use *will* and *you* in questions about what you want. Adhering to the volition-obligation distinction, the English usage guru Henry

112

Fowler pretty much admits defeat before he even starts a doomed attempt to squeeze the *shall/will* genie into a bottle in his seminal book *The King's English*:

It is unfortunate that the idiomatic use, while it comes by nature to southern Englishmen (who will find most of this section superfluous), is so complicated that those who are not to the manner born can hardly acquire it; and for them this section is in danger of being useless.

Yep. Perhaps even southern Englishmen have given up on *shall*, since its territory has been gradually encroached upon by other verbs.

One of the simpler auxiliaries is *may* (from Old English *mæg*) with its preterite *migh-t* (from *mih-te*) both now useable in the present tense (see 1.4 and 1.5 for *ght* in preterites). Its Old English meaning of *be able* has been refined somewhat in modern English, but the noun *might* meaning *power* recalls the basic sense of potency. A form of this exists as the Greek *mēkh-os* (μῆχ-ος - a *means* of doing something), which yields *mēkh-anē* (μηχ-ανή i.e. *mach-ine* and *mech-an-ical*). German's version of *migh-t* is used in polite requests – "Ich *möch-te* ein Eis" (I would like an ice cream).

The weak preterite of the Old English preterite present *āg-an* (to *owe*) is *āh-te*, which keeps its sense of obligation in its modern form *ough-t*. The past participle was *āg-en*, an adjective which became the modern adjective and verb *own*.

4.4

Little and often – diminutives and frequentatives

Dribbling and *nibbling*.

I have given suck, and know
> How tender 'tis to love the babe that milks me:
> I would, while it was smiling in my face,
> Have pluckt my nipple from his boneless gums,
> And dasht the brains out, had I so sworn as you
> Have done to this.

So says Lady Macbeth in her gruesome if effective pep talk to warm her husband's cold feet in the face of murder. Let's put the infanticide aside and focus on the *nipple*. Where did it come from? There is a common Germanic word for *beak* or *nose* which turns up in Danish as *næb* and Dutch as *neb*. This becomes *nib* in English where it has a more restricted use meaning *the point of a pen*. In 2.7 we saw the formation of diminutives in Latinate languages using a suffix which turned *femina* into *femella* and *vagina* into *vanilla*. English also formed diminutives using suffixes, one of which became *–le* in the modern language. A small *nib* is therefore a *nip-ple*. As for diminutives, a *nozz-le* is a small *nose* but I don't think *dong-le* is a diminutive of anything.

This suffix also appears on frequentative verbs, so to *nip* something repeatedly is to *nib-ble*. Due to the swapping of the *b* and *p* sounds, we *nibb-le nipp-les* rather than *nipp-le nibb-les*. The *nip > nibb-le* pattern is also seen in *drip > dribb-le*. To *wade* repeatedly is to *wadd-le*, as used by Juliet's nurse in this nostalgic conversation with Lady Capulet in *Romeo and Juliet*:

She could have run and *waddled* all about

On similar lines *stride > stradd-le, wag > wagg-le, daze > dazz-le* and *tweak* (Old English *twicc-an*) had an alternative form *twink* which formed a frequentative *twink-le*. This is used in the Old English translation of *The Consolation of Philosophy* in a conversation about God:

þēah   þū mē tǣhtest   ǣr   þā duru ac ic hire ne meahte
Though you showed me (before) the door (yet) I to it could no

māre āredian, būtan þ ic hire grapode ymbūtan þ þe ic þæt
more come,   but   I   it   groped   about   where I that

*lytle lēoht geseah **twinclian**.*
little light saw   **twinkling**.

Notes

Quotation from Laurence Sterne *The Life and Opinions of Tristram Shandy, Gentleman.*

Introduction
p.1
Stephen Pinker's *The Language Instinct:* – *The Language Instinct, How The Mind Creates Language* (New York: William Morrow, 1994).

languages being squeezed out of existence: See, for example, Suzanne Romaine and Daniel Nettle, *Vanishing Voices, The Extinction of the World's Languages* (Oxford: Oxford University Press, 2000).

the academic pursuits of the soldiers: A good recent account of this period and its characters can be found in Robert Irwin, *For Lust of Knowing: The Orientalists and Their Enemies* (London: Allen Lane, 2006).

Sanskrit may one day be taught: At the time of writing, Sanskrit is, I believe, currently taught at the London-based St. James group of private schools and the Krishna-Avanti faith school near London.

"A knowledge of Gothic": Walter William Skeat, *The Gospel of Saint Mark in Gothic: According to the Translation Made by Wulfila in the Fourth Century* (Oxford: Clarendon Press, 1888), p.viii.

p.2
pathologically eccentric obsessives: There is no shortage of examples. Two of the most magnificent are the Sanskritist Fitzedward Hall and the extraordinary English phonetician Henry Sweet, both of whom played vital roles in the production of the original *Oxford English Dictionary*. Hall's life is briefly and entertainingly recounted in Simon Winchester, *The Meaning of Everything – The Making of the Oxford English Dictionary* (Oxford: Oxford University Press, 2003). Sweet is superbly portrayed by George Bernard Shaw in his preface to *Pygmalion*, and provided some inspiration for the character Henry Higgins in the same play.

criminally ignorant: Bill Bryson, *Mother Tongue: The English Language* (London: Penguin, 1990).

Eskimos have lots of words for snow: Geoffrey Pullum, *The Great Eskimo Vocabulary Hoax and Other Irreverent Essays on the Study of Language* (Chicago: Chicago University Press, 1991), pp159-171. Pullum begins by narrowing the estimate to between two (the number of roots listed in Schultz-Lorentzen's 1927 *Dictionary of the West Greenlandic Eskimo Language*) and infinity, depending on how you define "Eskimo" (which is not a language), "word" (an English-speaker can normally choose one of two forms of a noun, singular or plural, whereas an Eskimo can choose from far more before you even start counting compounds and derivatives; besides, the structural differences between such languages and English allow the interpretation that the number of words for *snow* equates to the number of sentences in English which could include the word *snow*), and "snow". He settles on about a dozen. English has more words for rain, depending on how you define "English", "rain" etc. (yawn….), a fact which is unlikely to be anywhere near as fascinating to Eskimos as the snow myth seems to be to us.

there was no shortage of idiots: Mark Sanderson, review of Bryson's *Down Under* in the London Evening Standard.

p.4
Richard Salomon quotes: Richard Salomon, *Indian Epigraphy* (Oxford: Oxford University Press, 1998), p.3.

p.5
where Noah's ark came to rest: *Genesis* 8.4: "Then the ark rested in the seventh month, the seventeenth day of the month, on the mountains of Ararat."

Nineveh was thoroughly sacked: This was 'foreseen' by the unfortunately named Hebrew prophet Nahum the Elkoshite, who tells Nineveh in his vituperative Old Testament book that, "the voice of your messengers shall be heard no more". (*Nahum* 1.13) He didn't foresee Austen Henry Layard.

p.6
accidentally incinerated: Plutarch, *Life of Caesar* 49.3.

in the Afghanistan-Pakistan border region: See Richard Salomon, *Ancient Buddhist Scrolls from Gandhāra – The British Library Kharoṣṭhī Fragments* (London: The British Library, 1999).

p.7
"All religious strife": *Non aliunde dissidia in religione pendent quam ab ignoratione grammaticae.* Quoted in J.H.Groth, "Wilamowitz-Möllendorff on Nietzsche's *Birth of Tragedy*", in *Journal of the History of Ideas 11*, Apr.1950, p.188.

touch us as individual readers: Petrarch, who had a vital role in the recovery and study of the classical texts which stimulated Renaissance thinking, wrote: "Books delight to the marrow of the bones, speak, consult, and in a vital and acute way are united with us." (*libri medullitus delectant, colloquuntur, consultant, et viva quaddam nobis atque arguta familiaritate juguntur*) in *Epistolae de rebus familaribus et variae*.

p.9
First Germanic Consonant Shift: A good summary of this can be found in Don Ringe, *From Proto-Indo-European to Proto-Germanic* (Oxford: Oxford University Press, 2006).

p.14
the first Siamese: Pictures of this nominally seminal animal are plentiful on the internet.

p.15
entry for the word *tiffin*: Henry Yule and A.C.Burnell, *Hobson-Jobson, The Anglo-Indian Dictionary* (Ware: Wordsworth Editions, 1996 reprint), p.919.

Part One
p.17
Chinese whispers: If you are particularly sensitive to Sinophobia, please cross this out and write instead the game's French name – *le téléphone arabe*.

1.1
p.18
***manno tres filios assignant*:** Tacitus, *Germania* 1.2.

1.2
p.22
the Gothic stem *háubid-*: The stem-final sound represented here by *d* is actually a voiced dental fricative like the initial sound in English *that*. This occurred when intervocalic, such as in the genitive singular *háubidis*. In the nominative singular (and, being a neuter noun, the identical accusative) the fricative is devoiced before the inflectional ending *s*, like the initial sound in *thin*, and is written as *th* e.g. *háubiths*.

p.23
"Give me that man": *Hamlet*, Act III Scene II lines 76-78.

***one who has a good heart*:** Our English word *friend* has similar connotations, deriving as it does from the present participle of the verb *fre-on* meaning *love*. *Fre-on* is itself related to the Sanskrit root *pri* which occurs in Indian personal names such as *Pri-yā*, meaning *beloved* and reflecting the European name *Ama-nda*, the feminine gerundive of the Latin loving verb *ama-re*. I'm going a bit tangential here, but *priya* appears in rock inscriptions from the time of Aśoka, the third century BC Mauryan Emperor of India, whose discovery of pacifism unfortunately occurred only after he had done away with ninety-nine of his siblings and orchestrated the massacre of – by his own account – a hundred thousand people in the Battle of Kalinga. A series of rock inscriptions (possibly the earliest evidence of writing in South Asia) commemorate in a range of Prakrit dialects (Sanskritic vernaculars) his merciful conversion to Buddhism. These refer to him by a compound translatable as *beloved of the gods*. Spellings vary according to the regions where the inscriptions are found, but, for example, in the Gandhārī version of the eighth rock edict surviving in the village of Shahbazgarhi in the Khyber Pakhtunkhwa region of Pakistan (formerly known as the Northwest Frontier Province) the form used is *devanaṃpriya*. The word *deva* meaning *god* has the genitive plural ending – *nam*, giving the meaning *of*. The form of the compound is distinctive because Sanskritic languages tend to elide case endings from all members of compounds except the last – that is one of the efficiencies of compounding. It enables us to write *devapriya* as one word, but the rock scribe sticks the two fully inflected words together in an example of an *aluksamāsa*, a compound (*samāsa*) without (*a*) elision (*luk*) of the inflectional ending. All this is by way of precursor to pointing out that this compound in Sanskrit, as well as meaning *beloved of the gods*, can also mean *idiot*. Similarly in English e.g. "He forgot to put his trousers on again, God love him!" The best easily obtainable edition of the Aśokan inscriptions is Jules Bloch, *Les Inscriptions d'Asoka* (Paris: Les Belles Lettres, 2007).

1.3
p.26
"There is one expression"…."I select at random": Otto Jespersen, *Growth and Structure of the English Language* (Leipzig: B.G.Teubner, 1912).

p.27
"The feminine in Sanscrit": Franz Bopp, *A Comparative Grammar of the Sanscrit, Zend, Greek, Latin, Lithuanian, Gothic, German and Sclavonic Languages Vol.1* (London: Madden and Malcolm, 1845), p.126.

*für einen Augenblick***:** *Fleetingly*; literally, *in an eyeblink*.

is positively lewd: This is completely untrue. I have uncovered nothing remotely lewd in Bopp's lexical research (although I haven't read it in German).

p.28
in *mouse* (< *mūs*): *Mūs* appears virtually unchanged in Greek *mus* ($\mu\hat{v}\varsigma$), Latin *mus* and Sanskrit *muṣ* (मुष्). The word also occurs as a Sanskrit verb meaning *steal* and the rodent may have acquired its name from its naughty habits. The Latinate diminutive form is *mus-cle*. Do yours quiver like mice? The Sanskrit *muṣ-ka* (मुष्क) – *little mouse* – means *scrotum*. Does yours, oh, never mind…

119

George Bernard Shaw would have: GBS had no more joy in his quest for spelling reform than he did in one of his other ambitions articulated thus during a particularly severe attack of modesty – "With the single exception of Homer, there is no eminent writer, not even Sir Walter Scott, whom I can despise as entirely as I despise Shakespeare when I measure my mind against his. It would positively be a relief to me to dig him up and throw stones at him."

p.30

Sanskrit grammarian Pāṇini: The name is pronounced *Parninny* and has nothing to do with a cheese sandwich that looks like it has been run over by a burning car. His algorithmic system of four thousand rules describing the workings of Sanskrit is one of the greatest intellectual accomplishments of all time. Linguistic analysis did not come close to such intensity again until the mid-twentieth century. It should also be noted that these four thousand rules were not written down but memorised. As a leading Pāṇini scholar once remarked to me, "Writing was for dummies."

rephonologization: See Jerry Norman, "Pharyngealization in Early Chinese" in the *Journal of the American Oriental Society 114*, pp.397-408.

p.31

the verb *feed*: *Fōd-* derives from **fād*, which corresponds to Greek *pat-(πατ-)*, the verbal stem meaning *feed*. The Latin form of the verb, *pa-sc-ere* has a past participle *pa-st-*, which yields the English *past-or* (literally a *feeder*, hence the sense of *shepherd*, hence its application in denoting a member of the clergy.) This same root supplies the French *pain – bread –* which takes a prefix to form *com-pan-ion* and *com-pan-y*, people you take meals with (and in the case of *company* pay your *sal-ary*, cognate with *sal-t*).

1.4
p.32

"Although the series": Joseph Wright, *A Primer of the Gothic Language* (Oxford: Clarendon Press, 1892), paragraph 105.

p.33

the root **pet* meaning *fly*: In Greek this verb can mean both *fly* and *fall*. The latter meaning is seen in the zero-grade form in *sym-pt-om*. Its Sanskrit form *pat-* shares this double meaning. In fact, in Sanskrit it can mean virtually anything.

1.6
p.44

"Hail native Language": Opening lines of *At a Vacation Exercise in the Colledge*.

"Thou whoreson zed!": *King Lear*, Act II Scene II line 64.

p.45
"the *quick* and the dead": *Acts* 10:42; *1 Timothy* 4:1.

Part Two
2.1
p.50
"*On Cȳres dagum*": From an extract in *Sweet's Anglo-Saxon Primer* (Oxford: Clarendon Press, 1953; originally published 1882), rev. by Norman Davis, p.67.

"*And ælc mann*": Ibid., p.78.

"*Þanaseiþs izwis*": From an extract in Joseph Wright, *A Primer of the Gothic Language*, p.189.

p.51
"*dondezhe vidyet*": Quoted in S.C.Gardiner, *Old Church Slavonic – An Elementary Grammar* (Cambridge: Cambridge University Press, 1984), p.92.

his-tory (*ἱσ-τορία*) from **hid-tor-*: This *st* < *dt* is common, also seen in the Latin noun *ros-trum* < **rod-trum* meaning *beak* or *prow*. It has a basic sense of *pecker* from the root *rod-* meaning *gnaw* or *peck*. The current use of *rostrum* for an elevated platform derives from the name of a speaker's platform near the Roman Forum on which were mounted the *rōstra* of warships captured in the Battle of Antium in 338B.C. The victor in a sporting contest who stands on the top step of the rostrum, or the head of the pecker, can thus be said to occupy the position of peckerhead.

2.3
p.56
Known as the *Bhaṭṭikāvyam*: Alternatively as the *Rāvaṇavadha*.

a couple of obtainable English translations: The first by G.G.Leonardi (Leiden: E.J.Brill, 1972), contains the indecent squatting. The second, and better, by convicted manuscript thief Oliver Fallon must be unique among this sort of literature in acknowledging in its preface the support given to the translator by the inmates of Pentonville. My review of the Fallon edition (New York: Clay Sanskrit Library, 2009) can be found on the Sanskrit Literature website www.venetiaansell.wordpress.com.

p.58
A Greek noun: This does not mean that a pleasure-seeking *hēd-onist* is so called because they like sitting down. The long root vowel distinguishes *hēd-onism's* origin from that of *hedos* the *seat*. Our false friend *hēdus* (*ἡδύς*) is an adjective – originally *wadus* (*ϝαδύς*) - meaning *sweet*. Actually it is the word

sweet, which occurs in Old English as *swēte*, Sanskrit as *svādus* (सुवादुस्) and Latin as *suavis*, whence *suave* and *per-suade*.

2.5
p.64
"hēr bēoþ oft": From *Sweet's Anglo-Saxon Primer*, p.88.

meregrotan: *Meregrota* is the anglicised form of Latin *margarita*, and the word also appears in Persian as *murwarid* (مروارید) all meaning *pearl*. From this derives *margarine*, which is kind of pearly, and the name *Margaret*.

p.65
what's a whelk?: The subject of these particularly predatory molluscs whose purple anal excretions were so valued by the ancients as dye is certainly absorbing. However, it is possible to think too deeply. The Greeks had a verb for thinking deeply. *Kalchainō* (καλχαίνω) means *I search for the purple fish*. Would that we had created a similar association in English, we could say when deep in contemplation that we are *ferreting for a dogwinkle*, or something.....

"were like two full moons": *King Lear*, Act IV Scene VI lines 72-73.

p.66
"Jah warth skūra": *Mark* 4.37. From Walter William Skeat, *The Gospel of Saint Mark in Gothic*, p.10.

a place where there is a farm: P.H.Reaney, *The Origin of English Place Names* (London: Routledge and Kegan Paul, 1960), p.135.

2.6
p.67
"gesāwon ðā": *Beowulf*, ed. C.L.Wrenn (London: Harrap & Co., 1953), line 1425.

2.7
p.70
"Ārīs": *Beowulf*, ed. C.L.Wrenn, line 1390.

p.71
a different way in Urdu: This term is attested in V.T. Oldenburg, "Lifestyle as Resistance: The Case of the Courtesans of Lucknow" in *Feminist Studies*, 1990. For comments explicitly associating the name of this bread with lesbian sex see the extract from Devadatta Shastri's *Jaya* Hindi commentary on the *Kāmasūtra* quoted in the Doniger/Kakar English translation of the *Kāmasūtra* (Oxford: Oxford University Press, 2002), p.xxxv.

2.8
p.74
"because by fire": *1 Corinthians* 3.13.

2.9
p.78
"And Elde anone": From William Langland, *Piers the Plowman*, ed. Walter W.Skeat (Oxford: Oxford University Press, 1886), B.Passus XX lines 182-183, vol.1 p.589.

2.11
p.82
of the field: Further east the ancestors of the Ancient Greeks and Romans did not look earthward for their acorns, but upwards to the trees. Hence the Greek word for *acorn*, *bal-an-os (βάλ-αν-ος)*, related to the Latin *gla-n-s*, whose meaning is unlocked by the Sanskrit verb *glai* (ग्लै) meaning to *fall* (see 1.6 for further exploration of the *g/b* interchange). The *glans* of the male anatomy is thus so called because of its resemblance to the falling fruit of the oak tree. As the saying goes, "From little acorns..."

"Get you gone": *A Midummer Night's Dream*, Act III Scene II lines 326-328.

meaning *together:* For example the Latin *co-gno*, which supplies English with words such as *co-gn-ition* and *in-cogn-ito* is fully **cum-gno*. This answers directly to the Sanskrit *sam-jñā* (संज्ञा), meaning *understand*. The verb that appears in Latin as *gno-* and Sanskrit as *jñā-* is the English *kno(w)* (see 4.3 for more on this root).

Part Three
3.1
p.87
"Nor would we": *MacBeth*, Act I Scene II lines 70-72.

p.88

rule 1.1.45: *igyaṇaḥ samprasāraṇam* (इग्यण: संपरसारणम्) - Briefly translated, this means that in certain instances in place of the the semi-vowels *y*, *v*, *r* and *l*, represented in encryption by the word *yaṇ*, there are the corresponding vowels *i*, *u*, *ṛ*, and *ḷ* (the latter two do not occur as English phonemes), represented in the rule as *ig*. The replacement of the former by the latter is termed *samprasāraṇam*. An example of this is the *v* of the Sanskrit verbal root *svap* (स्वप्) becoming *u* in the past participle *sup-ta* (सुप्त). *Svap* means *sleep*.

"as every good Englishman": Skeat was short of neither humour nor genuine admiration when he commented on the preponderance of German scholarship in English language studies. In the introduction to his *Chaucer – The Minor Poems* (Oxford: Clarendon Press, 1888) he writes: "Mr Sweet has given us a few extracts from these, in his Second Middle-English Primer, but confesses that he has not 'attempted to forestall the inevitable German, who, it is to be hoped, will someday give us a critical editon of Chaucer.' Though I am perhaps to some extent disqualified, as being merely a native of London, in which city Chaucer himself was born, I hope I may be pardoned the temerity of attempting something in this direction." (p.vii) The Mr Sweet he refers to is the Oxford phonetician noted above.

3.3
p.94
"Go, bind thou up": *Richard II*, Act III Scene IV lines 29-31.

p.95
it connotes *auberge*: This is not originally a French word but a Germanic one. Or two, to be exact. In modern German we find the verb *be-her-berg-en*, the –*her-ber-* of which occurs in modern English as *har-bour*. After the prefix *be-* the element *–her-* is that found in Gothic *harj-is* and Old English as *her-e* and means *army*. The next element *–berg-* is related to the Gothic verb *baírg-an*, which occurs in Old English as *beorg-an*. These mean *preserve*. The verbs' vowels are altered in the related nouns to give Gothic *baúrg-s* and Old English *burh* or *burg* meaning a *protected place*. These nouns are ancestors of the modern German word *Burg* (*castle* or *district*) and English *borough*. A related development in Old English was the verb *byrg-an*, which becomes modern English *bury*. So, a *har-bour*, or without the *h* an *au-berge*, is basically a safe place for an army. The English form *har-bour* is not only a noun, but a verb meaning *protect*.

"The neighbours unanimously declared": E.W.Lane, *An Account of the Manners and Customs of the Modern Egyptians ed.1860*, p.307 (available at www.archive.org).

3.4
p.96
But that I am forbid": *Hamlet*, Act I Scene V lines 13-20.

p.97
***neque mittatis*:** We may have misunderstood these words from the Sermon on the Mount. This could mean, "Send sausages now and lard later." See above note for more on *margarita*; and 1.2 for more on words for *dog*.

Part Four

4.1

p.99

Þā wæs heal: *Beowulf*, ed. C.L.Wrenn, lines 1151-1153.

p.100

amēn qiþa izwis: From an extract in Joseph Wright, *A Primer of the Gothic Language*, p.145.

p.102

And ānum hē: From an extract in *Sweet's Anglo-Saxon Primer*, p.64.

ac hīe gesittaþ: F.A.Blackburn, *Exodus and Daniel: Two Old English Poems* (London: Heath & Co., 1907; available at www.archive.org), line 443.

kwam at marein: From Walter William Skeat, *The Gospel of Saint Mark in Gothic*, p.17.

As stars with trains: *Hamlet*, Act I Scene I lines 117-120.

4.2

p.106

the declension of the word for *table*: See Winston Churchill, *My Early Life* (London: Thornton Butterworth, 1930). If being able to address furniture seems a bit unnecessary, M.R.Kale went to another level altogether in his *Higher Sanskrit Grammar* (Delhi: Motilal Banarsidass, 1972; first published 1894.) After saying, "There are no words ending in ṝ or ḹ" he goes on to fully decline two imaginary words ending in these sounds, "to show what the forms of such words will be, if there be need to use such words." (Paragraph 84).

4.3

p.110

Iþ kunþēdeiþ mik: From an extract in Joseph Wright, *A Primer of the Gothic Language*, p.186.

p.111

xšnāsātiy tya adam: Inscription DB I.52 as reproduced in R.G.Kent, *Old Persian Grammar Texts Lexicon*, 2nd ed. *American Oriental Series no.33* (New Haven: American Oriental Society, 1953), p.117.

yesterday I perambulated: Would that the potential of the Latin verb *ambulare* had been better exploited by the addition of more diverse prefixes. Others were. Take *iacere* meaning *throw* – prefixes to its past participle *iect-* produce *sub-ject*, *pro-ject*, *ab-ject*, *re-ject*, *e-ject*. Why has *ambulare* been neglected? In addition to *per-ambulate* (*walk through*) we could have:

super-ambulate   = *walk over* or *trample*

hyper-ambulate = walk excessively (*hyper* is the Greek form of Latin *super*)
sub-ambulate = walk under
hypo-ambulate = not walk far enough (*hypo* is the Greek form of Latin *sub*)
pro-ambulate = walk in front of or *approach*
pre-ambulate = to make a false start in a walking race
de-ambulate = walk away
re-ambulate = walk backwards or *return*
ex-ambulate = walk out of
in-ambulate = walk into
dis-ambulate = walk defectively or perhaps *limp*
anti-ambulate = walk in the other direction
ambi-ambulate = walk around
inter-ambulate = walk between
post-ambulate = follow or *dawdle*
trans-ambulate = walk across or perhaps *mince*

p.112
Fráuja, jabái wileis: From an extract in Joseph Wright, *A Primer of the Gothic Language*, p.147.

Ic Ælfrīc wolde: From an extract in *Sweet's Anglo-Saxon Primer*, p.78.

p.113
"It is unfortunate that": H.G. and F.W. Fowler, *The King's English* (Oxford: Clarendon Press, 1908)

4.4
p.114
"I have given suck": *Macbeth*, Act I Scene I lines 54-59.

"She could have run": *Romeo and Juliet*, Act I Scene III line 37.

p.115
"Þēah þū mē tǣhtest": *King Alfred's Old English Version of Boethius De Consolatione Philosophiae*, Walter John Sedgefield (Oxford: Clarendon Press, 1899), C.xxxv.3.

Author's note on sources

This book was begun on the northern edge of the Libyan Sahara in a place referred to in Virgil's Aeneid as *inhospita Syrtis* – when, by a coincidence of wordplay, I happened to be working *in* a *hospital* in *Sirte* - and was completed in part of the Arabian Desert bordering the Empty Quarter. Accessing research material from these locations was not the work of a moment. I have endeavoured to ensure that sources are correctly cited. If anything has been overlooked I will be happy to rectify it immediately.

www.ingramcontent.com/pod-product-compliance
Lightning Source LLC
Chambersburg PA
CBHW030132260626
47156CB00008B/2903